WIVENHOE PARK

WIVENHOE PARK

Ben Vendetta

Thanks Nicolas!
Enjoy the book

COOPERATIVE TRADE
an imprint of Cooperative Press

WIVENHOE PARK

ISBN 13: 978-1-937513-30-6
First Edition
Published by Cooperative Press Trade, an imprint of Cooperative Press
www.cooperativetrade.com

For information about licensing, custom editions, special sales, or
academic/corporate purchases, please contact Cooperative Press:
info@cooperativepress.com or 13000 Athens Ave C288, Lakewood, OH
44107 USA

Join the Cooperative Press Trade email list at
http://eepurl.com/DS-m1

CONTENTS

Into You Like A Train 7

Thompson Twins From Iowa 13

Christine 21

Mirror In The Bathroom 31

We Could Send Letters 39

Meat Pies and Chip Butties 41

Alcoholiday 49

Nick Danger 59

Naked Pushups 69

You Trip Me Up 75

I'll Melt With You 79

Hit The North 87

The Boy Looked At Johnny From NYU 97

English Rose 105

Hanging On The Telephone 111

Making Plans For Julie 113

Don't You Want Me Baby? 117

Under A Blood Red Sky 121

What She Said 133

Too Cash 137

Mushy Peas In Paris 143

Staring At The Frat Boys 147

The Killing Moon 153

Roman Holiday 159

Beverly Hills Punk 163

Velocity Girl 175

Wivenhoe Revisited 181

There Is A Light That Never Goes Out 185

Someone Somewhere In Summertime 189

INTO YOU LIKE A TRAIN

It's been a month since Christine left me for the singer in a jumped-up local rock band called Saved By Zero and I still can't decide what irks me more; my adversary, Darren, or the fact that his group is named after a Fixx song. He struts around like the second coming of Simon Le Bon in padded blazers, elfish red vinyl boots, and a preposterous bleached blonde hairdo. I remember Christine once quipped that Darren probably took a picture of Daryl Hall to his hairdresser for inspiration, but now the joke's on me.

I'm with PJ at an end of fall term punk and new wave theme party at a sorority house, trying to forget this all went down. Though we're invited, at least PJ is—he deals a lot of weed to the Greeks on campus—the two of us look out of place, even with more than half of the revelers in costume. I'm wearing jeans, a black and pink Psychedelic Furs t-shirt, and a black leather jacket. PJ, who looks like a Say No To Drugs campaign anti-hero with shoulder length locks and three-day stubble, is sporting ripped 501's, a Violent Femmes t-shirt, and an olive green army jacket; marijuana leaf patch sewn on his left shoulder, upside down American flag on the right.

A lot of the girls in attendance are wearing brightly colored 'punk' wigs; a few even fastening safety pins through crocodile and polo player logos, as if that simple gesture is enough to transform themselves from preppy to punk. The guys are more clueless, favoring faded jeans, plain white t-shirts, and misguided bandanas, somehow duped into thinking that Bruce Springsteen, and not Johnny Rotten, is the rightful Godfather of punk.

The whole scene is making me uncomfortable. I hate fraternities. I've always preferred to have a few close friends rather than a bunch of casual acquaintances to have mundane conversations about drinking beer, cheating on exams, pulling trains on intoxicated girls, or whatever else frat guys like to gab about. Small talk makes me uneasy and occasions like this reek of it.

PJ leaves me to make the rounds with his girlfriend Caroline. She's a rebellious rich chick from Grosse Pointe and even has a gold nose ring to prove it, but that's not the only thing that violates said orifice on a regular basis. The two of them have been doing way too much blow lately. After a line or two it's a given that PJ will start acting like a dick and I can handle that. PJ's likeable even when he's an asshole. Caroline, on the other hand, just gets bitchy, bringing out her true country club colors. By the time she's thirty she'll probably be married to some attorney and having brunch with hubby and her parents every Sunday at the club.

As much as I hate to admit it, though, she is really hot. I can see what PJ sees in her, at least on a superficial level. She looks like Phoebe Cates with her long brown hair and tonight she's in a black leather skirt, fishnets, and a Clash t-shirt. Right now she's in good spirits, unlike a few weeks ago at a yacht club party in Grosse Pointe.

PJ and I had made the road trip from Ann Arbor into the heart of Detroit's most exclusive blue blood suburb, the two of us pounding a twelve-pack of Stroh's on the drive down. I was pretty sloshed when we got there, knowing full well I shouldn't have let PJ drive in that state, but was too shell-shocked over the break up with Christine to care much. When we got to the party, I continued to feed my buzz, knocking back several Seven and Sevens at the bar while PJ and Caroline disappeared to do coke and God knows what else. PJ has told me stories about her kinky side, like giving him blow jobs with cough drops in her mouth and even asking him to handcuff her a few times.

I hung out at the bar and bought several drinks for

Caroline's younger sister, Jackie, who was home from boarding school for the Thanksgiving holiday. She's a cute brunette who looked like she walked straight out of *The Preppy Handbook* in a plaid skirt and Ralph Lauren sweater, but it was immediately apparent that she took after her sister in the girls behaving badly department. We slinked off to a nearby conference room to make out, but didn't get too far before one of the chaperones caught us, just as I was reaching second base. The battle axe shamefully escorted us back to civilization as PJ and Caroline were simultaneously making their way back to the bar, sniffling their noses as if they had sinus infections. Caroline scolded me for taking advantage of her kid sister and started a huge argument with PJ. PJ decided he had enough and told her she was "harshing his mellow," so the two of us wandered off in the snow and proceeded to get lost once we got out of the confines of Grosse Pointe and into the mean streets of Detroit. We navigated our way through a landscape of abandoned buildings, boarded up homes, pawn shops, liquor stores, and even an abortion clinic, running every red light we came across to avoid getting jacked by groups of young men staring at us with crack cocaine eyes. We finally found refuge at a Church's Fried Chicken that was miraculously still open. We toked up in the car and giggled, somehow convinced that we were eating fried carp and not chicken. Soon after, I blacked out and didn't wake up until PJ's car rolled into Ann Arbor at the crack of dawn.

Right now I feel the urge to reach a similar state of intoxication. I worm my way through the crowd to the kitchen in search of this evening's cocktail of choice, grain alcohol punch. This batch is bright red, a similar shade to the volcanic lava one might expect to see in a Bugs Bunny cartoon. The atmosphere in the living room, turned makeshift dance floor, is pretty lively. While there's nothing remotely punk about the music pumping out of the obnoxiously large tower speakers, it's a non-stop hit parade of all the stuff I used to watch on MTV back in high school, and I'm secretly enjoying it. So far I've heard Duran Duran, Human League, ABC, Adam and the Ants, and INXS. I finish my drink and immediately knock back a refill.

I notice that this chubby girl, who looks like Kim Wilde with big teased blonde hair, is checking me out. It's pretty apparent that she's a sorority chick playing dress up, but it's feeding my ego even though I know she's not my type. She's wearing a baggy Frankie Goes To Hollywood t-shirt that says, "Frankie Say Relax" in bold black block letters, a short denim skirt, and pink Chuck Taylors. She comes over to say hi and asks if I want to dance, just as Modern English's "I Melt With You" kicks in. I've never been much of a dancer, but the punch is starting to work its magic and I take her hand. When Spandau Ballet's "True" comes on she leans over to kiss me. We start to make out and continue even when the sappy ballad fades into Billy Idol's "White Wedding," oblivious to everyone jumping up and down around us, fists pumping high in the air. When "White Wedding" simmers down she whispers into my ear, asking if I want to go upstairs.

I follow her up a staircase to her bedroom. She turns on a small bedside lamp, and, even though it's still pretty dark in there, I can see a lot of posters and pictures on her wall; Simple Minds, Duran Duran, Adam Ant, Psychedelic Furs, even The Smiths. An obvious giveaway to a privileged up-bringing is a series of three framed photos on her dresser: one of her posing with a group of smiling girls, all holding tennis rackets; one of her family, standing stern and upright in front of a yacht; one of her at a formal with a handsome all-American boy, presumably named Chip, Chad, or Brad.

She asks if I like Simple Minds. I say I do and she puts on their latest album *Sparkle In The Rain*.

"You look a little like John Taylor," she giggles as she runs her fingers through my shaggy brown hair. It would have been nicer if she had compared me to someone cooler, like Ian McCulloch from Echo and the Bunnymen, whose haircut I've tried to copy down to the exact detail, but now is hardly the time to complain.

We start to kiss as the opening strains of "Up On The

Catwalk" pump through the boombox speakers. She's too restless for foreplay and, after a minute or two, removes her t-shirt, unclasps her bra (before I even think of going there), and, actually, says she needs to get laid. I tell her that I don't have a condom, but she says that's not a problem. She's on the pill.

I nervously undress as fast as I can, half expecting her to suddenly change her mind. As I mount her, I lock eyes with a Psychedelic Furs poster above the bed that says, "Love My Way." I snicker to myself, thinking of a much cruder Furs song called "Into You Like A Train," which more than aptly describes my present predicament. I take a few deep breaths and try to keep beat, but by the end of "Book of Brilliant Things" she's already bored with missionary and sheepishly asks if I can climb off.

"It's easier for me to get off this way," she explains, as she presents herself to me from behind, her face now buried deep into a pillow. "Speed Your Love To Me" is on and my eyes rapidly scroll across the images of androgynous English pop stars on the wall, anything to distract me from speeding my love to her too soon. I can tell she's getting close. She starts commanding me to go harder and faster and I barely hold on, climaxing almost immediately after her, gazing into Morrissey's sad, disapproving eyes.

Afterward we just lie there and talk.

She says her name is Alison and I ask, "As in the Elvis Costello song?"

She smiles. She knows it. "You can call me Ali. All my friends do."

"My name is Andrew, but everyone calls me Drew."

She replaces Simple Minds with a Squeeze album, that greatest hits collection that everyone seems to own, except me. They're a little too happy-sounding for my tastes, but, obviously, I don't tell her that. I should feel ecstatic that I just got laid, that I'm back in the game, but I feel strangely melancholic.

Ali invites me to spend the night, but says she has to

get up early because she's flying home to Connecticut for the holidays. I say sure and we get under the covers. I ask if she wants to hang out when she comes back to Ann Arbor—suddenly, I feel lonely and crave the company—but she says she won't be here next term. She's going to spend the spring semester in Cambridge, England as part of a junior year abroad program. At that moment, one of those cartoon light bulbs flashes inside my head. Ann Arbor has been a real drag lately; Christine's not coming back and PJ's starting to become a total cokehead. I need an escape, even if it's just for a year. Ali dozes off while I lay awake fantasizing about living in England, seeing all of my favorite bands, maybe even hooking up with a cool British girl, one who won't break my heart like Christine did.

THOMPSON TWINS FROM IOWA

It's the first day of the following October and I'm on the way to the airport. I was hoping to get into the London School of Economics (after all, Mick Jagger briefly attended there), but ended up settling for University of Essex in Colchester, an hour train ride northeast of the capital, just off the coast, as close to London as an underachieving 3.0 GPA will allow. Immediately before the exit I see a sign that says, "Welcome To Romulus, Gateway To The World," proudly displaying the fact that the lifeless Detroit suburb's only claim to fame is an international airport, a portal to better places. Hopefully, it's a good omen.

My mom and dad are in front and I'm stretched out in the back trying to cop my best British rock star impression. I'm wearing my leather jacket over a Sisters of Mercy t-shirt, dark blue 501's, black Chuck Taylors, and a pair of Ray-Bans, even though I know it's starting to get much too dark for that. I packed lightly, strategically so, as if embarking on a tour of duty: a few pairs of jeans, an assortment of t-shirts, a black sweater, a few plain black and white dress shirts, a pair of Doc Martens and as many cassettes as I could cram into my suitcase's crevices.

My dad keeps reminding me that I'm going there to study and tells me to look up some professor he knew from his Oxford days. My mom tells me not to drink too much and keeps scolding me for not taking along a nice blazer in case I might get invited to some social functions. I laugh and say, "This isn't *Chariots of Fire*, mom. It's 1985."

I get along with my mom and dad OK, but, usually, I feel like the black sheep in the family. My dad is a professor and my mom is an editor for an academic press. If you've ever seen the TV series *Family Ties*, you get the idea. Like the Keatons, my folks are smug know-it-all liberals, whose opinions on life seem to be molded by public radio and *The New York Times*. It's not that I'm a Republican douche like their son, who is played by Michael J. Fox; I just see through their crap. My mom and dad talk about the horrors of teen pregnancy and drug abuse in the inner city, yet neither of them has ever asked me if I'm sexually active or do drugs. I can guarantee they never asked my older brother Paul.

Paul went to Princeton and now he's at Harvard, pursuing a Ph.D. He reminds me of angelic Kevin in the Undertones song "My Perfect Cousin" though his specialty isn't economics, mass physics, or bionics, but, rather, political science. He's been a straight A student his whole life and president of multiple student clubs and organizations. I'm the only one in the family that prefers sports to theater, rock 'n' roll to classical. In my world, Buzzcocks trump Beethoven, The Cure crushes Chopin, and Sisters of Mercy slay Tchaikovsky.

When we get to the international terminal, I feel a little like a kid getting dropped off at school for the first time. I've never really been away from home for more than a week (living in an on-campus apartment five miles from my parents' house doesn't really cut it). Paul went away for college but I opted to stay at home against my parents' wishes and accept a partial scholarship to run cross country and track at the University of Michigan. I start to feel a little nervous and scared, the same kind of jitters I used to get before a big race, and as if on cue I remove my shades. I say goodbye to my folks and remain on the curbside paralyzed, watching and waving until dad's trusty old Volvo wagon fades into the distance. I feel free, but it also feels weird.

Once inside I navigate my way through the terminal to the baggage check-in area, turn over my suitcase, and with my backpack slung over my right shoulder, make my way to the Pan Am gate. I have about an hour to kill before boarding the red-eye flight that should have me in London by 7:00am. A lot of the passengers seem to be my age, presumably heading off to an assortment of colleges and universities in the UK. Most seem pretty uninteresting; girls clad in sorority sweatshirts and Benetton tops, guys in button downs or Ralph Lauren polos worn with popped collars in an array of loud and obnoxious colors—on a quick, cursory glance I spot orange, lime green, yellow, and pink.

I notice two guys who stand out amongst the Reagan youth. One is tall with long blond hair, immaculately spiked and gelled on top like Mike Peters from The Alarm, while his counterpart looks like Tom Bailey, the singer from The Thompson Twins. 'Mike' is wearing a padded blue blazer over a horizontally striped black and white t-shirt, looking very much like an extra from Duran Duran's "Rio" video or maybe even Don Johnson's future sidekick in *Miami Vice*, while Tom is wearing a jean jacket over a Smiths t-shirt. They seem to sense a kindred spirit and walk over to me. Fabulous 'Mike Peters' turns out to be rather conventionally named Scott, while 'Tom' actually does turn out to be Tom!

They're both from Iowa State and will be spending the year in Wales. I immediately dub them the Thompson Twins from Iowa. This is just too funny! They light up when I tell them I'll be studying near London.

"That sounds so fabulous," gushes Scott, who is one of the more flamboyant guys I've ever met. "I wish we could have gone there, but our school has an exchange program with Aberystwyth."

"I imagine the architecture and history must be pretty cool, there," I respond, trying my best not to sound too elated that I'm not going to Wales. "Essex is pretty modern and dull looking from what I can tell, almost Soviet-like."

"But who cares, you'll get to see so many shows," says Scott. "Who are your into? I like your haircut. You look like you're in Echo and The Bunnymen or The Cure or something."

"Thanks. I love those bands, and Jesus and Mary Chain, Psychedelic Furs, Sisters of Mercy, anything dark and moody."

"I really dig The Jesus and Mary Chain," says Tom, who had been quiet until now. "I have their import singles."

"Me, too," I say. "My favorites are 'Never Understand' and 'Just Like Honey.'"

Scott sighs, "That video for 'Just Like Honey' is just so marvelous. They're lying around doing nothing, but they look so glamorous."

"What other stuff are you guys into?" I ask.

"I really love a lot of the New Romantic stuff like Duran Duran and The Human League," Scott says. "Oh, and I love Siouxsie and The Banshees. I really love Siouxsie Sioux," he gushes.

"I'd say my favorite band is The Smiths," says Tom straight to the point. "Morrissey is a genius."

Our conversation is interrupted by an announcement that we can finally board. I'm not seated too far away from Scott and Tom and I'd really like some fun company on this flight, so I trade seats with a frat jock dude who is sitting next to them. He seems incredibly relieved when I offer to switch. I later overhear him muttering something about 'damn Eurofags' to one of his buddies. I'm ashamed to admit to myself that a few years ago I actually hung out with guys like that. It's amazing how slight changes in hairstyle and clothing have somehow designated me as an outcast, a status that I pretty much welcome with open arms these days.

The on-flight movie is the most recent Bond flick *A View To A Kill*. I saw it in the theater over the summer, but it seems appropriate that it's showing here. It's pretty cool that Duran Duran got to do the theme song even though it's not nearly as good as their early classics like "Girls On Film," "Rio," or "Planet Earth."

The blonde stewardess, who looks to be on the north end of her thirties, asks if I want anything to drink so I press my luck and order a Jack and Coke. She asks if I'm twenty-one and I smile and say, "Almost." She laughs and says that in a few hours I'll be England's problem and gives me a pass. Realizing that they're now off the hook, Scott and Tom follow my lead and order screwdrivers. We sail through a few rounds and are feeling no pain as the three of us have an animated conversation about bands we've seen, bands that we wish we'd seen, and the general lack of culture in the Midwest. The conversation makes me feel incredibly grateful that I grew up in Ann Arbor and not Ames, Iowa.

"So do you play any instruments?" asks Scott.

"No, I don't seem to have any musical talent," I say. "I'm a music critic for my college newspaper though. I love to write. What about you guys?"

"I play bass and Tom plays guitar."

"We jam a bit," says Tom, "but haven't formed an actual band yet."

"Cool," I say.

"So who have you written about?" asks Scott.

I tell the Thompson Twins a tale about my first interview with The Sisters of Mercy, a conversation that kick started my journalistic aspirations. Sisters of Mercy were from Leeds, England and I had instantly connected with their heavy goth vibe. Their album, *First And Last And Always*, hadn't come out yet, but I had the "Alice" and "Temple of Love" singles and played them to death on my cheap Panasonic turntable. I managed to convince PJ to drive me to the show at St. Andrew's Hall in Detroit, even though it wasn't his scene at all. PJ makes friends wherever he goes, so I wasn't too worried about him not having a good time.

At the club PJ immediately made himself scarce and started hanging out with some guy near the backstage door. I assumed that he was negotiating a deal, maybe even selling weed to the band. I was too focused on the concert to really care. I could barely see the group on stage due to the fog machine cranked up to eleven, just black silhouettes in the distance, looking almost non-human; vampires with guitars, lurking in the shadows. The show was pretty mesmerizing as The Sisters of Mercy slashed and burned through all their classics, as well as a killer encore rendition of The Velvet Underground's "Sister Ray." They even played a few songs that I didn't know, but would later recognize when the album came out. "Walk Away" was one that really stood out that night.

When the concert concluded, PJ came up to me and said, "That dude I was talking to is The Sisters of Mercy tour manager. I told him that you're a writer for *Spin* and that you want to interview the band."

"What the fuck?" was my less than eloquent response. "What if they find out that I'm not a writer?"

"You worry too much, Drew. No one is going to hunt you down for an unpublished interview. Besides, now you have a chance to do something more than scribble in that damn notebook of yours."

He had a point. All spring I had been keeping a music diary, diligently jotting down notes about the records I bought and the concerts I attended, secretly harboring fantasies that I actually wrote for *Spin*, *Melody Maker*, or *NME*.

PJ and I went backstage. As soon as we entered the room, it felt as if we had been swept into an opium den or the headquarters of some secret society. Decadence and vice was in the air. The room was dimly lit and when my eyes adjusted, the first thing I saw were some barely legal goth girls in fishnets and lace openly doing lines of coke off an Elvis Presley album cover, strategically placed on a table, empty bottles of Jack Daniels and half-eaten sandwiches messily strewn about. The tour manager made the obligatory introductions and PJ offered everyone some weed, which nicely broke the ice. The Sisters of Mercy were all wearing black leather (jackets and pants) though the singer, Andrew, and the guitarist, Wayne, were tricked out in some pretty wild paisley shirts. They never removed their shades.

My questions were embarrassingly generic at first, as my nerves got the better of me from the lack of preparation. I was winging it on fear and alcohol. When I asked Andrew about his influences, he bluntly responded that the only three bands he liked were Mötorhead, The Stooges, and The Birthday Party. I told him that The Stooges were my favorite band and for the next half hour the two of us had an animated conversation about Iggy Pop, which abruptly ended when one of the gothic vixens slithered over and sat on Andrew's lap.

"Is that enough for your story, mate?" asked Andrew, after taking a long drag from his cigarette.

"More than enough, man," was the best I could say.

The drive home was a total adrenaline rush. My minor fantasies of becoming a journalist and living the rock 'n' roll high life in London, New York or L.A. just had a microscopic dose of reality.

"You know if you write that article, I could get it published for you," said PJ.

"So you're dealing weed and publishing magazines, too?"

"No, man, but Mark, the music editor for *The Daily*, buys from me. The dude is a total pothead."

I excitedly pieced together a small feature on The Sisters of Mercy which zeroed in on Andrew's admiration for The Stooges and the thrill of playing in Iggy's old stomping grounds. Mark dug the piece and published it in one of the last issues of the spring semester, telling me to hook up with him in the fall for more assignments.

After telling the Thompson Twins this story, I'm dying for a piss. I excuse myself and head over to the John, trying not to stagger out of the aisle. When I'm done, I splash some water on my face and pop a Valium. I don't take Valium all that often, but love the trippy buzz it provides when mixed in with a few cocktails.

When I get back to my seat Tom is passed out and Scott starts gabbing about how he's already missing his girlfriend. He shows me a picture of a cute girl with bleached blonde hair and an asymmetrical haircut, who looks maybe eighteen at best. He asks me if I have a girlfriend. I say no but it feels more complicated than that. I still carry a photo of Christine in my wallet even though it's been close to a year since we broke up. I ran into her just a few days ago and I've been a total wreck since, just as I was hoping to start the year with a clean slate.

CHRISTINE

I met Christine just after I started college and began crushing on her almost immediately. She worked at Schoolkids' on Liberty Street, the best record store in Ann Arbor, the only one that carried the cool independent releases, including all the British imports. Christine had jet-black hair done up like Siouxsie Sioux and dressed head to toe in black, her wardrobe contrasting nicely with a ghostly pale complexion. I wanted to ask her out but kept freezing. In high school all the girls I knew were super preppy, but Christine looked like she had arrived from another planet, or at least London. After a few months the two of us managed to become friendly enough that she would recommend records that I would immediately, and, perhaps too eagerly, purchase in order to impress her. I tried to play it cool but always felt clueless and cumbersome in her presence. I even started drinking coffee as an excuse to hang out at Drake's, a cool smoke filled sandwich shop with a film noir-like décor that she and her friends often frequented. PJ and I would sometimes see her at concerts, but we would never manage to exchange more than a quick hello. I was dying to get to know this girl.

PJ was my best friend when we first started high school. The two of us ran cross country and track together and I still have fond memories of hanging out in PJ's basement bedroom, geeking out over the latest issues of *Runner's World* and *Track and Field News*, talking about the colleges we planned to run for. He wanted to go to Villanova, for me it was always Michigan. The two of us drifted apart junior year after he became a full blown party monster and stopped taking running so seriously, while I made All-State for the first time. PJ didn't even run senior year and the two of us now only occasionally crossed paths at parties where I might have a quick token beer before making an early exit because I had to run the next day.

PJ and I reconnected at a frat party just after I quit the Michigan cross country team. We had something in common again, former runners in search of less than natural highs. He was bigger than me, standing a few inches over six feet and had put on some weight after he quit running. His once conservative cropped hair was now shoulder length and he was wearing ripped jeans and a Che Guevara t-shirt. PJ let it slip that he'd been doing a little dealing on the side and the two of us got stupidly high that night, so much so that I still vividly remember chasing around a cricket on a sidewalk, convinced that if we smoked it we would get even more baked. Later that evening PJ kept telling a sorority girl that raisins were God's cure for hangovers.

It was amazing how much I changed after just three months of college. For as long as I could remember, my only goal in life was to be a star athlete. First it was baseball, but when I concluded that I would never be more than a decent fielding second baseman with a batting average south of the Mendoza line, I took my best shots at basketball and soccer. I could shoot and kick, but I couldn't dribble or maneuver worth a damn in either sport. I could run laps though, very well in fact. I was always teased for being too skinny, so I started doing what a lot of skinny guys did and joined the track team in eighth grade. Within a few months I could run faster than a five-minute mile and won the city middle school meet. In high school I continued to excel and even won a few state championships before it was all over.

When I started running for Michigan, I learned in a hurry that while I was good, I wasn't quite as good as I thought, certainly not skillful enough to train hard and party even harder like the legendary Steve 'Pre' Prefontaine, whose poster graced my bedroom at home, and now the dorm room

I shared with a teammate. For the first time in my life I had zero adult supervision, succumbing to a twenty-four hour party lifestyle like so many other freshmen. A few beers on a weekend in high school became at least a few every day. The drinking and over training was turning me into a nervous wreck. As my running performance started to slip and my coach started to question my dedication, I started to have panic attacks, so much so that a school counselor gave me a prescription for Valium. At the end of the season I asked the coach if I could skip track season and come back to the team in the fall; I always preferred cross country to running circles around the oval anyway. He said I could if I didn't want my scholarship anymore, so I quit. It was a pretty minimal stipend, just for books and a fraction of tuition, but it was an achievement that even my non-athletic parents seemed proud of.

The Valium helped with the anxiety and blues, but the drug that really got me over the hump was rock 'n' roll. I always liked music when I was a kid, but for the most part it was never much more than background noise, listening to the radio in my bedroom or cranking up The Rolling Stones and Led Zeppelin when I borrowed my dad's car. Just a typical Midwestern hard rock loving boy until an older friend I knew from the running scene opened up my eyes and ears to a brave new world.

Richie was in his mid-thirties when I met him the summer before my senior year of high school. He lived a few blocks away from my folks. He was a very successful runner on the local scene in addition to being a legitimate rock star back in the day. His early-Seventies hard rock band from Detroit had a couple of minor hits, one of them would later get covered by a famous L.A. hair metal band at the end of the Eighties and throw him back into the limelight. Now Richie was in AA and running was his only drug. When we'd run shirtless in the summer I'd always gaze at the faded needle scars on his wiry, ripped arms. Richie had long shaggy blonde hair and I started to grow out my hair to be like him. Friends thought I was copying rock star runners like Pre, Nick Rose, and John Walker, but Richie was the guy I wanted to be like the most.

I would go running with Richie on weekends when I wasn't practicing with my team and he'd tell me amazing stories about the other Detroit bands he played with back in the day like The Stooges and The MC5, even Bob Seger back when he was cool. He taped me a bunch of stuff, too. I instantly fell in love with The Stooges and Iggy Pop. When David Bowie's *Let's Dance* album became the soundtrack of choice at seemingly every party I went to my senior year, I would always try to remind anyone within earshot that Iggy Pop's version of "China Girl" was superior.

With running suddenly out of the picture I spent all of my free time obsessing over new music discoveries on left of the dial radio stations and through an assortment of music magazines. *Rolling Stone* was OK, *Spin* was much better, but I spent most of my cash on British publications like *Melody Maker, NME, Sounds,* even *Smash Hits*. The teen-oriented *Smash Hits* was a guilty pleasure. Before long I was a full-fledged Anglophile, buying albums by The Cure, Echo and The Bunnymen, Psychedelic Furs, The Smiths, and many more.

I tried to dress the part, too. In high school and at start of college I looked like a cross between a preppy and a stoner. I wore the obligatory khakis, but my hair was on the longish side thanks to Richie's influence, and I was too lazy to iron or tuck in my button down shirts. Now I lived in black and blue Levi's, replaced my K-Swiss sneakers with Chuck Taylors, and started wearing a lot of black t-shirts, some plain, others displaying images and logos of newly discovered bands.

One afternoon in May, a few weeks after that Sisters of Mercy show, I was hanging out at Drake's, admiring the cover art of The Cult's recent twelve-inch single "Spiritwalker" that I had just bought. Christine had told me about them. The singer Ian and guitarist Billy used to be in a band called Southern Death Cult, now they were just The Cult and much more rock 'n' roll than goth. Christine wasn't at Schoolkids' that day, which bummed me out, but I bought the record anyway. A few minutes later I looked up and saw her having coffee with a group of friends at a table nearby. She waved to me and, somewhat shockingly, came over to say hi.

She said she heard that I was the guy who wrote the article about The Sisters of Mercy. Suddenly, I was the guy.

"Are you doing anything tomorrow?" she asked.

"No. I have the day off." Back then I was washing dishes at a popular lunch spot not too far away from Schoolkids' named after a Seventies AM radio hit about an afternoon quickie.

"Do you want to hang out?"

"Sure," I said, trying as hard as I could to stay calm.

"How does noon here sound?"

"Perfect."

The next day we hit a few used record stores, including one that Iggy used to work at. Afterward we went to a Chinese restaurant where we started to gaze at each other lustfully, or, maybe in retrospect, it was just me. The cryptic fortune cookie message seemed optimistic at the time, "Dream your dream and your dream will dream of you." In any case, I was smitten. I had gone out on dates in high school, but nothing remotely serious. This was the first time that I felt really vulnerable in a girl's company. She asked where I lived and I told her that the apartment I shared with PJ was nearby.

She then asked if I wanted to drink or get high—*of course I did*—so the two of us stopped at a seedy grocery store near my apartment. Christine picked out a moderately expensive bottle of red and said something about an old boyfriend liking this particular brand. I cringed a little at the mention of a past flame, hopefully not visibly, but regained some composure and confidently broke out the fake ID PJ scored for me, a Florida driver's license that told the world I was a twenty-two year old from Sarasota named Sean Guckin.

The place I shared with PJ was the lower level of an old rundown house. It was a small two-bedroom apartment, with a living room, kitchen and scuzzy bathroom (shower, no tub). I moved there from the dorms at the end of April when school got out. PJ's old roommate flunked out during the spring semester and wouldn't be returning in the fall, so his room was mine for as long as I wanted it.

I found two clean glasses in the kitchen and luckily there was a corkscrew lying around, which I didn't know how to use too well. Christine did and had it open as fast as a restaurant maître d'. We took the bottle and glasses to my room, which was wallpapered with music posters and concert flyers to mask the peeling white paint. I asked Christine if she wanted to listen to anything and she flipped through the stack of records on the floor before putting The Cure's *Seventeen Seconds* on the turntable. After a few sips of wine, the two of us started to make out.

"You're a virgin, aren't you, Drew?"

"Jesus, is it that obvious?"

"No, it's just that I can tell you're really nervous. Lie back on the bed and just relax."

I did as she said, while she unzipped my jeans and went down on me. "This way you'll last longer when we do fuck," she said between heated breaths.

I didn't know what to think—this was such an alien sensation—so I just closed my eyes and enjoyed the ride. Dear *Penthouse*... After I climaxed, she laughed and said, "Let's take a shower before I take your cherry."

Christine was pretty skinny, like a lot of the girls I knew from my running days though thankfully she was more amply endowed. We made out some more in the shower and it didn't take too long for me to get aroused again as I lathered her perky breasts with Irish Spring. When we got out she took my hand and led me back to bed, guiding my actions as if I were a novice artist tackling a paint-by-numbers project. This time I was more relaxed, my initial anxiety fully iced by the wine buzz and soon, but not too soon, I was no longer a virgin.

"Not too bad at all for a first time," Christine laughed.

"I've had some guys finish almost as soon as they've started."

I went to the kitchen and brought back a few beers and we spent most of the evening in bed just talking. Christine graduated from high school the same year that I did, but while I went to a private school full of professors, doctors, and lawyers' kids, she was from blue collar Ypsilanti just down the road. She said she was always getting into trouble at school and in ninth grade started hanging out with an older crowd of punk rock kids. Her dad was AWOL, but the one good thing he had done before bailing out on his family was leaving behind a lot of good records, so Christine grew up on stuff like The Beatles, Stones, and The Who.

"So is your family really rich?" she asked.

"Pretty well off I guess. My dad's a professor."

"So have you ever been abroad to England or anywhere in Europe?"

"I've never been to England, but I've been to places like Paris and Rome."

"I'm so jealous. I've never been out of this damn state. So are you going to be a writer when you graduate?"

"I hope so. My parents want me to go to law school but my grades aren't really that great. Writing is the only thing I really like to do. But who knows? A year ago, I wanted to be in the Olympics."

"For what?"

"Running."

I got out of bed and grabbed a scrapbook from my dresser, which was full of news clippings from my glory days.

"My dark secret," I said as I handed her the book. "I used to be a jock."

She flipped through the scrapbook and said, "That's really cool. I like a man who's got a passion. It doesn't matter what for. Do you still run?"

"Not too much, maybe once a week if I feel really stressed out."

"So are you passionate about anything other than music?"

"Just you," I said as I leaned over to kiss her.

The two of us became pretty inseparable after that. She'd stay with me more nights than not and on days that PJ was around we'd hang out with him and Caroline, drinking and getting high. At the end of the summer I was convinced beyond doubt that I loved her and told her so.

That day is still vividly cemented in my mind. It was Labor Day weekend and we were in her bedroom at the apartment she shared with her mom near the Ypsi/Ann Arbor border. The complex stunk of divorce and single parenthood. You know the kind of place. Every town has them; basic, inexpensive cookie cutter units with broken Venetian blinds, carport garages, and a decrepit communal swimming pool. I had never been to Christine's apartment before, but her mom was out of town for the evening and she wanted to make me dinner. She made a pasta dish that was quite excellent—I had no idea she could cook so well—and now we were now drinking wine in her bedroom.

The room was small but it was amazing. Posters of Bauhaus ("Bela Lugosi's Dead" cover art), Echo and The Bunnymen (*Ocean Rain* cover where they're on that boat in the cave), The Cure, and Depeche Mode graced her walls. She had tons of records; a bunch of old ones that her dad left behind, plus all the latest UK independent releases that the two of us bonded over. I remember wondering how the hell she could afford to buy so many, even with her store employee discount. She still kept some of her toys from childhood around, too, like stuffed animals and Dr. Seuss books. It showed a softer and sweet side that I always wanted to see more of.

I told her how much I liked her room.

"Thanks, Drew. I like it, but I feel like I'll never leave this place."

"What do you mean?"

"I feel like I'll never be able to move out. In a few years you'll be done with school and making a lot of money and I'll probably still be working in retail."

"I'll take care of you. You could live with me," I said.

"That's really sweet, Drew, but it's too early for you to really mean that."

And that's when I poured my heart out. I told her that I was madly in love with her, couldn't imagine a life without her, and that I'd take a bullet for her, pretty much all the shit that usually worked in a John Hughes movie. She was pretty blown away, but shot me down gently, saying she wasn't ready for anything that heavy. She said I was 'too nice' and 'too good' for her, things she had told me before and I instantly regretted opening up.

That day proved to be a turning point in our relationship. The decline wasn't sudden, but, over the coming weeks, I could feel Christine slowly slipping away. Christine and I would still hook up in the fall, but with much less frequency. The sex was still good—at least to me—but the emotional connection had waned. We weren't spending enough time together for it to be much more than a casual arrangement. She decided to go to beauty school to get a cosmetology license—she figured she might as well make money at it instead of cutting all her friends' hair for free—and when I'd call she'd either not be around or in a hurry to get me off the phone. Instead of letting my first love run its natural course, I fought the decline every step of the way.

Seeing Christine less and less fed crazy thoughts into my head. I started getting jealous, and, she, in turn, seemed to get off on that, casually mentioning guys who were interested in her, like a girl cheerfully tearing off flower petals. He loves me, he loves me not. All I knew was someone named Darren was getting brought up too damn often to just be a 'friend' and I was ultimately proven right. Saved By Zero had a record release party for their seven-inch single at small club in October and Christine and Darren first hit it off there. I was too busy at the bar drowning out the awful music to pay attention to Christine playing musical chairs right under my nose.

"He's actually a really nice guy," she said. "I think you'd like him."

At first I put up with it, hoping this infatuation would

pass, but one day, just before Thanksgiving, she said that we should see other people. When a girl says those words it can only mean one thing; I've found someone else and I'm going to start seeing him, deal with it. As far as I was concerned, she may as well have already slept with Darren. I knew it was over and I was devastated. Those words—"I want to see other people"—pummeled me like a powerhouse punch to the gut. I blew up and half yelling, half crying, called her a fucking slut. She called me a jealous psycho and we stopped speaking, just like that.

MIRROR IN THE BATHROOM

A few weeks later I hooked up with Ali and followed through on my drunken self-promise, filling out several applications for junior year abroad programs in England. I knew LSE was a long shot, but the guy in the Study Abroad office pretty much guaranteed I would get into Essex, telling me that it was a really strong university for the Liberal Arts. Even though it was still months away, I was starting to get really excited. I was now visualizing myself at clubs I had only read about—The Marquee, 100 Club, Electric Ballroom—and I started paying closer attention to the latest fashions, desperately wanting to fit in with the right crowd when I got there.

I even bought a Union Jack to put up in my bedroom. I knew I wouldn't take it with me to England—that would have been absurd—but I wanted to play the part, just like a method actor prepping for a big role. I was listening to a lot of The Jam, Billy Bragg, and The Smiths that spring—the most 'English' bands in my collection—paying special attention to lyrics about Eton rifles, rains falling down in humdrum towns, Saturday boys, and pretty girls who made graves.

"Pretty Girls Make Graves" always reminded me of Christine. Years later, it still does. It took a long time to get her out of my system and I compensated by having a few more meaningless hookups, including an eighteen-year-old Deadhead from Pennsylvania named Sunshine, who ended up crashing at our apartment for a few days on her way to San Francisco, and a girl I barely knew from the cross country team, who had somehow heard I had become a heroin addict. More bizarrely, she found that intriguing. I think I assured her that I wasn't, but I only slept with her once, so who knows what she ended up telling people?

The writing was going really well, the one part of my life that was really shining. I had become *The Daily*'s go to guy for articles and reviews on British bands and some of the cooler American groups like R.E.M. and The Long Ryders, spending much more time on my new avocation than studying or going to class. In April I got accepted into Essex and as elated as I was, it was really tough going to Mark's office at *The Daily* and telling him I wouldn't be around in the fall.

When school got out, I decided to move home to save money. I wasn't hanging out with PJ much anymore. He was doing way too much coke and spending a lot of time with a new crowd of delinquent rich kids. PJ never pressured me to party, but he almost never called, so I got the message.

My summer was boring, which in a way was a good thing. My mom landed me a job doing grunt work for her publishing company. I worked in the mail room, unloading boxes on and off of trucks and drove around a lot, picking up envelopes from graphic designers and dropping off proofs to printers. It beat washing dishes and it paid more, too. I tried not to spend too much money on records and when I did buy them, I made sure to write detailed reviews of every purchase in order to keep my writing sharp.

I even started running a few days a week with an old Michigan teammate, Keith. I stopped getting high so much and was amazed at how good the lungs felt again. Keith lived in a house with several other guys on the team and I began to hang out with them once or twice a week, renting dumb action movies like *Red Dawn* and *Rambo* and knocking back beers. Most of the runners would automatically stop after two or three, other than an Australian guy named Craig, who drank like a fish and kept me company.

Keith was running about seventy miles a week and seemed destined to make the varsity squad. I was a little jealous but also very proud. I was faster than him when we were freshmen, but now, just two years later, he was on his way to scoring a varsity letter. I watched the team's time trial on the first Friday in September. It was a five-mile race on the University of Michigan golf course. The grass there is immaculately manicured, but there are several brutal hills and twists and turns that make it one of the more difficult Big Ten courses. I remember it being eighty-five degrees in the shade that afternoon as I tried to stay as cool as possible, enviously watching the twenty-five or so lean and ripped runners perform their final stride outs. Everyone was shirtless, scantily clad in nylon running shorts and spiked shoes. I was still thin but my ribs no longer stuck out so much and my abs weren't as defined as my former teammates'. I didn't miss the grueling interval workouts on the golf course, the weekly hill repetitions on the even tougher Huron Hills golf course, and the dry heave-inducing six-mile time trials through the steep and winding Barton Hills neighborhood, but I did miss days like this, when we were fully tapered and ready to push our bodies to the limit.

The top two runners, both All-Big Ten performers from the previous season, wasted no time, separating themselves from a tightly bunched group of about fifteen. They were running just under five-minute per mile pace and, even over the rolling terrain, it looked like a walk in the park for them. Keith was in the chase pack and looked really good. Several of the others around him were already struggling, hanging on for dear life, their form betraying them, looking more like runners in the final stages of a race. These guys were the hardworking walk-ons, high on desire but low on natural talent. They trained their asses off all summer for this one shot of glory, but soon they would lose touch with the main group and watch their dreams painfully slip away, their bodies rejecting their noble aspirations.

Three miles in and Keith was running smoothly in sixth place, increasing the distance on the seventh place runner by at least fifty yards. He had a pained expression, but I could almost see a trace of a smile on his face. He was going to do it. He ended up catching one more guy and made the varsity squad with ease. That evening I had a few beers with him and in all seriousness he told me he was worried about me and hoped that I would take care of myself in England.

"You know, you have a redshirt year of eligibility left, plus your senior year. If you get in shape while you're in England, you could come back to the team and run for us."

For a minute or two I contemplated the idea. As early as my sophomore year of high school I had dreamed of wearing a University of Michigan letter jacket, and it really wasn't so farfetched of an idea, but in my heart I knew I wasn't that guy any more. I said goodbye to Keith and headed over to the upstairs room venue of the Heidelberg German restaurant on Main Street to see a new band I'd heard good things about called The Laughing Hyenas.

I got to the club and within a few minutes I ran into a kid I went to junior high with who was now a total new waver. His haircut was pushing Flock of Seagulls absurdity levels. After some initial chitchat, he asked, "Hey, Drew, are you going to see Howard Jones at Pine Knob next weekend!?"

He spoke with the zeal of an A&R man who had just discovered The Sex Pistols in a seedy basement club, but in this case, Howard Jones was your typical one-hit wonder from across the pond that MTV played ad nauseam along with Dead or Alive, shared haircuts and all. When I said no, he almost seemed dejected.

Later I ran into PJ, who I hadn't seen all summer, and was quite shocked at his transformation. Most of his hair was chopped off and now slicked way back. Not quite Don Johnson, but he was heading in that direction. He was wearing black designer jeans and a white v-neck, a screwdriver in one hand, Camel Light in the other. He was hanging out with a dude with blonde feathered hair named Danny, who was wearing flip flops, plaid Bermudas, and a beige t-shirt that said, "No Fat Chicks."

PJ bought me a beer. He was animated. "How's it going, man? When are you going to England?"

"Like three weeks."

"Fucking awesome, dude. I haven't seen you at all this summer, what's going on?"

"I've been mellow, just trying to save money for the trip. My mom hooked me up with a job."

"Good deal. That is if you have to work."

"I take it work is going pretty well for you."

"For sure, man, for sure."

The Laughing Hyenas were pretty solid. While they were a bit too heavy and scuzzy for my Anglophile sensibilities, they had a blues meets punk sound that brought to mind The Birthday Party, Nick Cave's old band. The gig concluded and I decided to bail. PJ and Danny had other plans.

"Drew, dude," said PJ. "The night is still young. Do you want to go to the Déjà Vu with us? It's amateur night."

"Sure, man."

Against my better judgment, I decided I would accompany them to a strip club in Ypsilanti. Might be the last time I hang out with PJ before leaving.

We piled into Danny's BMW, Tears For Fears booming on the stereo, and made our way to Ypsi. I had only been to a strip club once before—freshman year a few of us in my dorm went to a joint in Windsor, Ontario, ludicrously named The Beanery. The drinking age was only nineteen in Canada, but that place was so gross that even the access to legal beer wasn't worth it. There was nothing remotely sexy about the dancers up close; just a lot of cellulite, scars, and blank expressions.

The bouncer at the Déjà Vu was a dude I remembered from junior high named Rico. Back then he was a chubby little kid who loved disco. Now he was huge, well over six feet tall, and jacked up. His black hair was styled like John Travolta in *Saturday Night Fever* and his silk shirt was unbuttoned half way, exposing several gold chains. I thought the disco ship had sunk, but Rico was still bravely treading above water.

Rico didn't recognize me, which was fortunate. I still needed to be Sean Guckin for a few more weeks until I got to England and could drink legally. We took a seat, ringside, as an almost too-skinny brunette was finishing up her act, g-string riding up her ass, dollar bills sticking out in all directions like leaves on a tree, ripe for plucking. The MC, a stocky balding guy, who looked like Phil Collins with a mustache, walked up on stage, mic in hand.

"Gentlemen, welcome to the Déjà Vu!"

A crowd of Eastern Michigan University frat boys started howling, while the old blue collar men in attendance looked awkwardly down into their glasses of beer.

MC Phil Collins continued. "Next up is Roxy! She's a college girl from the school of hard knockers."

Roxy walked up to the stage. She was a short chubby blonde, who was indeed more than amply endowed.

"Roxy's getting a Ph.D., or should I say, Ph. Double D's!"

Phil started laughing at his own joke before hacking up phlegm like a lung cancer patient on life support. Fortunately, the DJ was alert enough to catch Phil's folly and after only a few seconds of awkwardness, Roxy quickly got down to business to the strains of Olivia Newton John's "Physical," immediately discarding her t-shirt and shaking her tits as men fed bills into her g-string.

I had already knocked back a few beers during the Hyenas' set and needed to relieve myself pretty badly at this point, so I headed to the can. After finishing my piss, and trying not to laugh too much at the graffiti above the urinal that said, "Desiree goes down for weed" (indicated with a downward pointed arrow), I walked over to the sink to wash up. PJ and Danny were coming out of a stall, giggling.

Danny had some blood on his t-shirt and was holding a piece of tissue over his right nostril.

"Drew, dude," said PJ. "Do a farewell to America line."

I had never done coke before and the thought of it never really crossed my mind, but I was feeling self destructive that night; something to do with watching the cross country time trial earlier that day and my post-race epiphany that I was no longer a runner. A part of my life had died, and a line of blow seemed like the perfect way to seal the deal.

"Sure, man," I said.

"Right on," said Danny. "Let's party!"

We went into a stall and PJ cut a comically large line on a small mirror that he removed from his pocket.

"Dude, that line is huge," said Danny.

"Fuck yeah," said PJ, "Only the best for my boy, Drew. He's going to do a Sam Kinison-sized line."

I pressed down my left nostril and took a huge hit with my right. My first impression after losing my cocaine virginity was that it felt like I had ingested ground up school board chalk, but it definitely enhanced my beer buzz.

Danny and PJ each did another line and the three of us decided to leave the Déjà Vu in search of real women. We walked over to a dive bar called The Wrong Number, PJ entertaining us along the way with quotes from Tony Montana, the drug dealer played by Al Pacino in *Scarface*.

"In this country, you gotta make the money first. Then when you get the money, you get the power. Then when you get the power, then you get the women."

"That's what I'm talking about," shouted Danny at the top of his lungs.

"And no fat chicks," I chimed in, pointing to Danny's t-shirt.

"Fucking A," said Danny.

After a couple of beers at The Wrong Number my enthusiasm started to wane. PJ had somehow remained calm, even after doing yet another line with Danny (I passed), but now Danny was out of control.

He pointed to some girls at a nearby table.

"See those girls?" he slurred as he wagged his right index finger at four sorority sisters, who were sharing a pitcher of beer. "Those girls are real sluts. They'd give us blow jobs for sure. They're total cum chuggers."

"Hey, we can hear you," said one of the less than amused co-eds.

PJ and I started laughing, but one of the gals walked

to the bar and within minutes, the bouncer asked us to leave.

"Don't ever come back to The Wrong Number," he said.

"We'll try not to, boss," said PJ, "But it's going to be tough."

We walked a few blocks through downtown Ypsilanti back to Danny's car, weaving around drunken college kids as if we were playing an intoxicated version of Pac-Man. Danny kept asking strangers to give him five, holding out his hand.

"Don't leave me hanging man, don't leave me hanging," he kept saying.

Danny said he could drop me off at my parents' house on their way back to PJ's. They still wanted to party. I was spent. PJ popped out the Tears For Fears cassette and switched to a hard rock station.

"I hate those fags," he said as he tossed the tape on the floor.

AC/DC announced to the world that they were "Back In Black" and then Richie's song came on, his big hit. I smiled, thinking of more innocent times, and that's the last thing I remembered until Danny woke me up in my parents' driveway.

WE COULD SEND LETTERS

A few days before going to Essex I stopped by Schoolkids' to say goodbye to some friends, and was startled to see Christine behind the counter. Her hair was no longer sprayed up like Siouxsie Sioux. It was still dyed black but it was now worn straight, just past her shoulders. I watched her walk over to help a customer. She was wearing leather pants, a sleeveless Mötorhead t-shirt, and a studded silver belt. She had replaced the big Gothic cross necklace she used to practically live in with a silver padlock choker; something that Sid Vicious might have worn. She still looked smoking hot. I wanted to say hi, it was the perfect opportunity for some closure, but I felt too numb to do anything except stand there and stare. She turned around and waved, just as I was ready to bolt. She yelled out to her boss that she'd be back in five and I followed her outside, not knowing what to say or what she might say.

We both started to say sorry at almost the exact same time, before I let her continue. She said she felt really shitty about how it all ended and that she wished she had stayed with me.

"I guess I was freaked out that day you said you loved me. No one has ever said that to me. You always said really nice things to me. I kept thinking you might call me, but you never did."

"I was too pissed off and crushed. What could I say? I knew you wanted to be with Darren."

"Oh god, that was such a nightmare. I went out with him like twice. He's a dick. You were right. I was too stubborn to admit it. I should have called you."

"It's OK. We're here now." There was an uncomfortable pause. I had nothing.

She continued. "I heard you're going to England. I'm going to miss you."

"I'm going to miss you, too," I said.

I unconsciously put my hand on her hip, before stopping myself. "Sorry," I said, "Old habits."

She laughed and said it was OK. "Look if you stay here much longer, I might not let you leave."

I couldn't tell if she was teasing me—she was always a huge flirt—but she did seem a little choked up, which surprised me. Part of me didn't trust her any more, but the less sensible side of me was already succumbing to her spell. So Darren was a douche after all? Part of me wished I hadn't given up on Christine, and then it dawned on me that maybe she liked me more at this moment because I hadn't been nice to her.

"Promise you'll write," she said.

I smiled and told her, "We could send letters," in reference to an Aztec Camera song on *High Land, Hard Rain*, a record that we often listened to.

She laughed and said, "You better," before heading back inside. As the doors opened I could hear "London Calling" blasting from the store speakers.

MEAT PIES AND CHIP BUTTIES

I wake up to an announcement that we'll be arriving in London soon. I'm nauseous from the drinks and Valium, but the adrenaline is surging. I'm really here! The plane lands and I navigate my way through customs with the Thompson Twins, saying goodbye after picking up my suitcase. I'm on my own now and need to take the subway (I soon learn everyone calls it the Tube) to Liverpool Street Station before catching another train to Colchester.

The first portion of the trip reminds me of an underground airport train I took with my family in Munich one summer when I was fourteen. Some of my best memories are from train rides. My dad and I were never that close, but one of my earliest remembrances is taking a trip with him and Paul from Vienna to Innsbruck when I was just four. We had lived in Austria for a year while my dad was on a sabbatical. I laugh out loud, remembering a picture in my mom's photo album of Paul and I wearing school uniforms consisting of shorts, shirts, ties, and blazers, looking very much like miniature versions of Angus and Malcolm Young from AC/DC.

After leaving the airport, the train goes above ground and the scenery becomes totally alien to anything I've seen. The houses, pubs, newsagents, and shops look almost too quaint to be real. I half expect this to be a movie set that will get torn down as soon as we go past. I wonder if Mary Poppins will fly by to let me know I'm still dreaming. I smile at that thought, remembering a time PJ and I did mushrooms on a weekend trip at a friend's cabin and thought that donkeys from a neighboring farm were trying to talk to us. The Tube goes back underground closer to the city and I get off at Liverpool Street, manage to find the correct train on a confusing electronic arrivals/departures board and hustle when I realize I don't have much time to spare.

Even though I'm exhausted, I'm way too excited to sleep. Leaving London, the train navigates its way past an endless succession of commuter belt towns and villages. The highlights are pretty minimal, the outposts being the English equivalents of the American middle class suburban dream, though I do note that Romford has a greyhound track, something I've never seen before. I watch the towns roll by (this must be what Morrissey meant by humdrum towns) while I zone out to New Order's latest album, *Low-Life*, on my Walkman; Stratford, Romford, Shenfield, Chelmsford, Hatfield Peverel, Witham, Kelvedon, Marks Tey, and, finally, Colchester. New Order was always the soundtrack of choice when I borrowed my dad's car and the band's sweeping atmospheric amalgamation of dance beats, shards of noisy guitar, and spooky bass lines proves to be an equally delectable tonic for this journey. From Colchester I take a cab to the university and am disappointed to discover that the ride takes us around the town instead of through the city center. Colchester is the oldest recorded Roman town in Britain. I remember that from a history class I had on the Roman Empire freshman year. The ruins will have to wait for another time.

The University of Essex looks exactly like the photos in the brochure that came with my letter of acceptance. It was built in 1963 and the buildings have a cold, almost Stalinist feel. Perhaps it's no coincidence that Essex was a hotbed for student unrest in the late Sixties and early Seventies. The architecture alone justifies armed retaliation. The surrounding greenery, however, makes up for it. The campus is situated on a picturesque hilly property called Wivenhoe Park, the subject of a famous nineteenth century painting by renowned landscape artist John Constable. Cows no longer wander freely on the countryside like they do in the painting, but the pond is still there, and swans, like the ones depicted in

Constable's piece, are frequent visitors. I've been assigned a room in Eddington Tower, on the south side of the university campus, just a short walk up a small hill from the main university square. It's Wednesday and classes won't start until the following week, but a lot of students are already here. Tomorrow, I'll have to suffer through an orientation with the other Americans.

My general impression of the students I see milling about campus is that they're trendier than Americans. The guys are all wearing cardigans or vintage looking blazers, as if they were extras in a Smiths video. A lot of the girls have dyed hair (blonde, black, red, even pink and purple) and wear leggings and skirts. Polo nation this is not. I can hear a few American voices and my first instinct is to say hello to fellow travelers before I remind myself that the whole point of this trip is to get away from that shit. I hope that everyone who looks at me assumes I'm English.

My room is on the fifth floor of Eddington, a fourteen-story tower that from the outside looks more like a housing project than a dormitory. Not Cabrini Green bad, but certainly not The Ritz. The layout inside is generic, too. There are sixteen single bedrooms on my floor, eight on each side, sandwiched by a common room and kitchen. My room is slightly larger than your stereotypical Japanese hotel room, with just enough space for a desk, a few shelves, and a bed that's about as comfortable as a motel cot.

It's lunchtime, at least my body clock is telling me that, so I decide to venture out and find a bite to eat. I'm too lazy to shower, but I wash my face, change shirts, and apply a new layer of deodorant. The old French spit and shine. I opt for an Echo and The Bunnymen t-shirt with the cartoon logo of the warped looking bunny creature that graced the covers of the "Pictures on My Wall" and "Rescue" singles. I stick with my black leather jacket and put on shades even though it's cloudy outside.

In the common space there are two guys talking and smoking cigarettes. One of them has his hair styled back into a glamorous pompadour like James Dean, with equally impressive sideburns. He's wearing a black cardigan over a crisp white thrift store dress shirt and a pair of cuffed jeans. His friend is dressed entirely in black and has spiky bleached blonde hair like Billy Duffy from The Cult. They look up and James Dean says, "Alright mate?"

"Hi, how's it going?"

"American, eh," says James Dean. "Nice t-shirt by the way."

"Thanks. I'm Drew. I just moved down the hall into room six."

"I'm Dave. I live in room two and this is Simon," he says, pointing to his goth pal.

I ask if there's a good place to eat and Dave says they're about to get a pint at the Union Bar and invites me to join them. The Union Bar is a large wide open space, more reminiscent of a moose lodge or a VFW hall than a proper pub, but the pints are super cheap, fifty to sixty pence a pop (less than a dollar). The food menu trips me up and Dave and Simon burst out laughing as they try to explain the intricacies of a Ploughman's, Shepherd's Pie, and a Cornish Pasty. I opt for the Shepherd's Pie, which is more or less ground beef, potato, and a few veggies backed into a pie crust.

I knock back a few pints of John Smith's bitter, which goes down smooth (extra smooth according to the beer mat I place my glass on in between sips). It's amazing how much better the beer is here compared to the Budweiser, Heineken, and Stroh's I usually drink at home. I learn that Dave and Simon are part of the Entertainment Society at Essex and they help book bands to play at the campus venue. They have already planned road trips to see The Cult in Ipswich in a few weeks and The Jesus and Mary Chain in Norwich in November. I commend myself for falling into the right crowd so fast and easily. I tell them about some of the bands I've seen and about some of the writing I've done.

Dave tells me that he knows someone at *Melody Maker* and asks if I have any clips I can give pass on to him.

This trip is turning out to be too good to be true. Simon says he wants to see my Sisters of Mercy article.

"They played at Essex last autumn," he says. "Just before they broke up."

"I wish I could have seen them again," I say. "I saw them in Detroit before *First And Last And Always* came out."

"I can't believe you lot like that rubbish goth shite," chimes in Dave.

"Who do you listen to?" I ask.

"I like groups with some intelligence, like The Smiths or bands with a socialist agenda. You know, like Redskins, Easterhouse, Billy Bragg, Style Council."

"Bloody leftie," says Simon.

"You can laugh mate," Dave says, "But Reagan and Thatcher are ruining the western world. I'd almost rather live in the Soviet Union than America."

I don't agree with that, but I'm certainly no fan of Reagan and American foreign policy. "Not everyone in America likes Reagan," I say. "I sure as hell didn't vote for him."

"Well that's good mate. I wouldn't speak to you if you had."

I can't tell if he's being serious or not, so I leave it at that and go to the bar. It's my turn to buy a round. It's not even dark outside and I'm quite buzzed. This could be a long year.

The rest of the evening quickly becomes a blur as more and more people join our table. Everyone in the bar seems to know Dave, who appears to be the big man on campus amongst the artistic set, the cock of the walk as the Brits used to say. Dave's crowd seems intrigued that I am an American and actually want to hang out with them.

"We get a lot of Yanks here," said one, "but they tend to stick together."

"Or hang out with the bloody Conservatives," said another.

The students here are politically aware. I don't know anyone at home who is remotely interested in politics. Most American college students just want to get drunk and laid. I had always naively assumed that Europeans liked Americans (after all we did bail them out in World War II!), but suddenly it doesn't seem so simple.

The next morning I wake up to a raging hangover and stink of second-hand smoke. Everyone here seems to light up nonstop. Even PJ, who got stoned all the time, rarely smoked tobacco. I remember chuckling like a junior high boy every time I heard anyone ask if they had a fag, which is UK slang for a cigarette.

I go to the kitchen and grab a couple of slices of bread from my shelf unit (everyone here gets an assigned locker to keep non-perishable items like bread, canned foods, tea, and coffee). Last night Dave gave me a spare loaf of bread and some Marmite that I'm about to experience for the first time. This should hold me over until I can buy some real groceries. I take some tea from Dave's shelf and boil some water. I'm definitely more of a coffee guy, but this will have to do.

It's 8:30am and everyone in the flat is sound asleep, recovering from drinking escapades and other tomfoolery last night. I met a few more flatmates when I came home from the pub, including a ginger-haired Scotsman named Alan who was slicing up potatoes like a madman and making everyone chip butties, a sandwich consisting of buttered toast, chips (French fries), and ketchup. Sober, I would have been appalled, but I remember now, just before passing out, that I proclaimed to anyone within earshot that it was the "best fucking sandwich ever."

I hazily remember that Alan had his boombox out while cooking and kept playing a French language version of Paul Hardcastle's huge hit "19," a song that was impossible to avoid all summer on MTV, the radio, or virtually any retail store I walked into. Alan was in a language program in Paris last summer and thought that this was the funniest thing he had ever heard. The song samples actual sound clips from war correspondents, like the one at the beginning that says, "In World War II the average age of the combat soldier was twenty-six, in Vietnam he was nineteen," followed by Hardcastle repeating, "ni-ni-ni nineteen, nineteen, ni-ni-ni nineteen, nineteen," over and over. The French remix naturally replaces "nineteen" with "*dix neuf.*"

I still have "*dix neuf, di-di-di dix neuf*" rapidly repeating in my brain as I take my tea and toast to the living room. I'm not alone. I see a stocky guy with short brown hair wearing a button down and jeans drinking orange juice. He says hi. An American. I say hi and ask if he's going to the orientation. He says yeah but that he'd rather be in bed. His name is Dan and he's from Georgetown. He says that he and few other guys from his school got in yesterday and went to the Top Bar, the other campus watering hole, which I later learn is where a lot of the conservative Brits and most of the Americans hang out. I tell him that I had a long night, too. He asks if I was part of the crowd making French fries. I plead guilty and proceed to tell him about chip butties and how I think I've lived to tell the tale.

Dan and I walk down the hill to the main square and go to a lecture hall where the orientation is taking place. There are about thirty Americans on campus. At least ten are from Georgetown, but the others are from a variety of schools, mainly small liberal arts colleges in the Northeast like Bowdoin, Williams, and Bucknell. No one else is from Michigan. When we get a break I find a vending machine that dispenses tea and coffee. I opt for the latter. Dan introduces me to a couple of girls from his school. They both have obnoxiously big hair and are wearing matching blue and gray Georgetown sweatshirts, smacking their chewing gum loudly in tandem. Christ, I may as well be back in Ann Arbor if I'm going to have to put up with this crap all year. After some polite chit-chat I excuse myself as fast as I can for a quick piss. I wash my face and try to straighten my hair though it does look kind of good. The combination of bedhead and a few days of stubble makes me feel like Bob Geldof. On the way back to orientation I see the Bobbsey twins filing in ahead of me, oblivious that I'm right behind.

One of them says, "What's up with the guy in the

leather jacket? He's a total Euro."

Her friend asks, "What's a Euro?"

"You know, a Eurofag. An American who acts like he's not."

Fuck you, I mutter quietly. I take this as a sign from above that I don't belong in a dreary lecture hall, listening to a smug limey administrator tell the Yanks about English life, and decide to head back to Eddington. I make a quick stop at the university store for food and toiletries and see issues of *Melody Maker* and *NME* on a shelf next to all the daily scandal sheets like *The Sun* and *The Mirror*. Despite *The Sun*'s promise of topless girls on page three, I only buy the two music papers. When I get to the flat Dave is up, making tea. I toss him the *NME*. He says, "Cheers, mate" and offers me a cup. The two of us spend the rest of the morning and early afternoon shooting the shit, drinking endless cups of tea, and reading both magazines cover to cover. Dave even reads some of my stuff from *The Daily* and says he likes it. We have time to kill before the pub opens.

ALCOHOLIDAY

I sail through my first month at Essex in a drunken haze, learning in a hurry that, unlike American universities, going to class here is pretty optional. The academic year at English universities is structured into three ten-week terms, separated with month-long winter and spring holidays. Students retain the same classes for an entire year, the only requirements being lengthy essays for each course, every term. As long as you can write and have solid research skills, you're pretty golden. My courses on Theories of Political Violence and Marxian Theory are really interesting and I attend most of those lectures and seminars. My Marxian Theory professor is really cool. He has a beard and smokes a pipe during seminars. My other two classes—Modern American History, which I thought would be interesting from a British perspective (it isn't) and Western European Politics—aren't as compelling and I tend to skip most of those.

I get to know some of the other people in the flat and they're a really fun bunch. Besides Dave, the guys I hang out with the most are Alan, the Scotsman with the culinary skills; Chris, an American music lover from Newcastle who digs The Long Ryders, Green on Red and R.E.M., and finds it funny that I like so many British bands; and James, a football (soccer) fanatic from Derby who is always up for a pint and a laugh. I get along well with Dan from Georgetown and hang out with him a bit (the two of us made a trip to Colchester the first week to buy cheap boomboxes), but I sense that most of the other Americans think I'm on the weird side. I feel much more at home with the Brits and quickly embrace their culture, attending football matches at Fourth Division Colchester United and nearby Division One club Ipswich Town, gigs and discos at the university's basement club, and endless pints at the Union Bar.

I've shared a few lighthearted postcards with Christine. I send her one of some Roman ruins in Colchester. She sends me one of downtown Ann Arbor and writes, "Iggy Pop misses you. So do I. Love, Christine." In the meantime, I've developed a small crush on an English girl I've seen around a few times. I don't have any classes with her and I haven't seen her at any flat parties, so my expectations are pretty low. She looks to be a few inches shorter than Christine, maybe 5'4", but with very similar features, namely dark hair and pale skin. Like Christine, she wears a lot of black though my English crush doesn't appear to be a card carrying goth.

One night at the bar I see Dave talking to my mystery girl and when he comes back to the table, I eagerly fish him for info.

"Her name is Julie," he tells me.

"So what's her deal?"

"What do you mean, mate?"

"You know. Does she have a boyfriend?"

"She did until really recently. He was a year ahead of us. They split up when he graduated. His name is Matthew. He's a pretty good bloke. They were together for a long time."

"So why did they break up?"

"Not sure, mate. I heard that she was going to drop out of university to move to London with him, but obviously something changed. Do you fancy her?"

"Yeah!" I try not to sound too eager.

"I can introduce you. She's a nice looking bird. I've always fancied her a bit myself."

"If you're interested, you should go for it. You knew her first." Obviously, I don't want this to happen but I'm trying to adhere to some kind of male code.

"Nah, it's OK mate. I don't want any rings or strings this year."

Later that evening Dave introduces me to Julie and adds, "He's an American," which comes out sounding funny, as if he was describing an exotic creature purchased at a high-end pet store. Fortunately Julie is pretty nonchalant and just smiles and says, "Nice to meet you." Before I can attempt any kind of conversation, several of her girlfriends steer her away and Dave and I go back to our table.

On the last Saturday of the month we go on a pub crawl to celebrate Dave's twenty-first birthday. The crawl is known around Essex as the Wivenhoe Run (Wiv Run for short) since most of the pubs are located in the neighboring village of Wivenhoe, just a mile or so up the road from campus. The Run involves drinking ten pints in the course of just four hours (British pubs open promptly at 7:00pm with last call being at the barbaric early hour of 11:00). The crawl commences at the Top Bar at the university, followed by a bus ride to the outer edge of Wivenhoe where you begin a journey back to the university on foot, hitting eight village pubs along the way, before literally having to run about a mile to make last call at the Union Bar.

About ten of us set off. Among them Dave, Simon, Alan, Chris, James, Dan, and a few others I don't know. The early rounds are easy as the pints go down smooth and everyone is having a good laugh. The pubs in Wivenhoe are cozy and quaint, more often than not with a fireplace, a nice change of pace from the factory floor feel of the Union Bar. I remember traditional names like The Station, The Greyhound, The Rose and Crown, and The Black Buoy. The punters are a mix of older couples having a quiet pint, working class lads having a piss-up, and casuals and soul boys in tight v-neck sweaters having a few before heading off to a nightclub to pick up tacky blondes in white heels and short skirts, the uniform of choice for every young girl I see in Colchester who is not a student.

Despite the rapid consumption of alcohol the group manages to behave pretty well until one of the guys I don't know, Nigel, loses it. Nigel has been going on all evening about shagging some of the African girls on campus, repeating the clichéd line, "Once you go black, you never go back."

At the last Wivenhoe pub on the crawl, Dave has enough and says, "Oi, wanker. So what's your secret for pulling all those black birds, then?"

Nigel unzips his jeans and whips out his cock and says, "You need a big plunker to please an African bird."

It's pretty big. I have to give him credit for that. Some of the patrons nearby look over at Nigel with horrified expressions. Nigel proceeds to slap his dick on an ashtray.

"You need a proper tool for a proper job," he continues.

Everyone starts laughing nervously until the barman comes over and promptly throws us out. "Oi, you lot are banned for life," he yells as we run out the door in hysterics.

A few of us have to piss and Nigel leads the way to a phone booth. Dan and I opt for some nearby bushes.

"We only have about fifteen minutes to get to the Union Bar," yells Dave. "I need to pick up a bird this evening and get a birthday shag."

We start running lightly for a few minutes before half of the group complains that they're already knackered. I'm pretty thankful. It hits home how out of shape I've become since the summer as we stumble along a dirt path through Wivenhoe Park to the university. I can't help but wonder what John Constable might be thinking from his grave as members of our entourage stop to urinate on the trees and bushes that he so lovingly depicted in his famous landscape.

Dan, who earlier in the evening told everyone he was an Eagle Scout, seems to sense the universal discomfort and boldly takes on leadership reins. He engages everyone in raunchy call and response chants he learned in the scouts and soon we're moving with precision along the dusky trail. I feel alert again. For a while I had been fighting the urge to pass out and was half tempted to nap next to a large tree that seemed to be calling out to me like the magical forests in *The Lord Of The Rings* trilogy. Soon we're at the Union Bar with a few minutes to spare, yet another pint of John Smith in my hand.

When the bar closes we go to a student disco that is

held in a vast, cavernous basement club. The club has an afterhours liquor license and sells overpriced cans of beer and cider. I buy a Holsten Pilsner for myself and another for Dave.

"Happy birthday!"

"Cheers, mate."

I notice Julie dancing with two of her friends; a slender redhead in jeans and a leather jacket, along with a short, chubby blonde in a Fifties rockabilly dress. Julie's wearing a long black skirt, a pink top, and a black cardigan, grinning from ear to ear.

"Let's join them," says Dave. "The night is young."

"I feel like the Dead Kennedys' song," I respond. "I'm too drunk to fuck."

"Suit yourself, mate. I'm a British bulldog," he replies as he grabs his crotch to further drive the point home.

The DJ is playing a decent selection of *Smash Hits* type music, nothing too edgy but definitely nothing mainstream. So far I've heard New Order, Fine Young Cannibals, The Cure's "Inbetween Days," and The Cult "She Sells Sanctuary."

Julie and the other girls laugh when they see the two of us stagger over to them.

"So are any of you going to give me a birthday snog?" asks Dave.

They just giggle.

"Come on it's his birthday," I plead as I hiccup. Smooth.

"You two are well pissed," says Julie.

"We lived to tell the tale," I proclaim. "Wiv Run!"

Dave and I try to dance with the girls for a few songs, but I'm really out of synch and feel like I'm just invading their space. I want to puke. A slower number comes on. I ask Julie to dance. She says no. I leave. She stops me and says, "Say hello to me sometime when you're not so pissed."

I don't know how to read this. I'm too wasted to think straight. Does she like me? Does this mean I have a chance? I decide to go back to Eddington and sleep it off. As I start to make my exit I run into Dan and some of his Georgetown buddies.

"Want a beer?" says Dan.

I hesitate for a few seconds.

"Sure," I say. Dan buys me a Holsten from the beer guy.

Suddenly a wave of depression encompasses me. I haven't written a damn thing since I've been here. Drunken, indecipherable notes scribbled after seeing The Cult a few weeks ago don't really count. Dave keeps telling me he'll send my clips to his *Melody Maker* buddy, who I'm starting to think is fictitious. I wonder what Christine is up to.

"Would it be a really bad idea if I called an ex-girl-friend?"

"Like right now?" asks Dan.

"Yeah."

"Not a good idea," says Dan's buddy Pete. "Nothing good happens on those kinds of calls."

I finish my beer and chat with the Americans some more. I ask if any of them have started their essays for the term. Some have, some haven't.

"This place is crazy," says Pete. "At Georgetown we'd drink on Thursdays and on the weekend. Here it never ends."

I'm a little hungry and debate going to one of the food trucks that's parked outside. The guys in my flat call them rat burger vans. The servers remind me of the carnies I used to see every summer when the fair came to town. Pock faced men with long, greasy hair and women in tight t-shirts, who look like a cross between biker chicks and the amateur wives you'd find in *Hustler* magazine's Beaver Hunt. My mind wins the battle with my stomach (no rat burger!) and I head up the staircase to the square and begin my excursion to Eddington before making a sudden, jerky detour to a little lobby that has payphones. I make sure I'm alone, piss against a wall, and go inside. I still have Christine's number memorized. I pull out the credit card my parents gave me for emergencies (this feels like one) and talk to the operator. Soon the line is ringing. I doubt she'll answer. It's 1:00am now, which means it's 8:00pm the night before in Michigan.

She picks up.

"It's me."

"Drew, is that really you? Are you OK? Did something bad happen?"

She seems really shocked to hear from me—after all, it is a late night transatlantic call—but I assure her that everything is fine.

"I'm glad you're OK then." She seems relieved. "It's nice to hear from you. I keep thinking about that last day you came to the store. I really wish we didn't go so long without talking."

"Me too."

"So what have you been up to? Are you still writing?"

"Not nearly as much as I should."

I tell her about my new friends and some of the concerts I've been to. She seems excited that I got to see The Cult.

"Do you ever miss me?" she asks.

"Yeah. A lot."

"That's sweet."

"You looked so hot that last day. I still get horny thinking about it."

She laughs. "If we hooked up that day, I might have never let you go."

"Tonight's the first night I wish I hadn't. I've been having an awesome time and all but we got really wrecked tonight and now I'm feeling really depressed."

"You'll be OK. You were always so ambitious when you were writing for *The Daily*. I used to love to watch you type. Promise you won't give up."

"I won't. So, what have you been doing?" I ask. "I had no idea you were back at the store."

"Yeah, beauty school really wasn't my thing. The only thing I seem to really like is music."

"Are you seeing anyone?" I bravely ask.

"No, nothing serious. You know me. I keep falling for

idiot boys in bands. Seeing you that last day just made me sad. Sometimes I wish I could go back in time. Are you coming home for Christmas?"

"No. I made some plans to visit friends here."

She sounds disappointed, but says, "That should be exciting. I wish I could come visit you."

"I wish you could, too."

Christine has to leave. She and some friends are going to see The Replacements, which surprises me since that's not her cup of tea at all, and I instantly imagine it's because of some guy she's interested in. I end the call feeling jealous and more alone than I was before phoning her. Next year Hüsker Dü would release a phenomenal pop song called "Don't Want To Know If You're Lonely" that perfectly nailed down how I felt at this moment. I don't want to know if you're lonely, Christine, and I certainly don't want to know if you're less than lonely.

I go back to the flat. Half of the people are already passed out. Others are eating chip butties or beans on toast. I get a glass of water and take it to my room. I put Aztec Camera on the boombox and fast-forward to the fifth song, "We Could Send Letters." It slays me every time. Roddy Frame is my age and he wrote it when he was only seventeen. It's a sad, dramatic account about how his girlfriend left him to go away to college. While the track has some nice jangly guitars that wouldn't sound amiss on a Smiths record, it feels more human and straight from the heart than anything Morrissey has written. Don't get me wrong, I love The Smiths, but sometimes Morrissey tries to be clever just for the sake of being clever. I play the song three times in a row and finally doze off near the finale as Roddy waxes poetic about finding blood he wasn't meant to find and finding feelings that he thought he'd left behind.

I wake up and feel sick as all hell. I can probably ride it out till morning, but know it's best to pull the trigger and be done with it. I go to the bathroom, kneel down, and stick my finger down my throat. On the first attempt I just dry heave, but the second time is the charm and I blow chunks and gross liquid spew into the bowl. I stay in the bathroom with my head over the toilet for a few more minutes until I know I'm in the clear before going to the kitchen for a large glass of water.

I can't sleep now so I lay awake in bed and think about Christine. I remember how I got really sick one night a few months after we started going out. We had gone to see Echo and the Bunnymen with PJ and Caroline and the four of us got pretty trashed that night. On the way home, PJ had the genius idea of stopping at a dive liquor store to get a bottle of Mad Dog. I already had way too much beer and a few hits of weed and, against my better judgment, took a big swig of Mad Dog, immediately regretting it. Without warning I had to throw up. PJ was racing down I-94 at like 85mph, but somehow I managed to roll down a window and puke out a glorious rainbow that flew backwards high in the air, before splattering the windshield of the car behind us. Christine and Caroline were pretty horrified, but PJ and I couldn't stop laughing. The moment was so surreal.

I managed to stay collected for the rest of the drive, but once we got back home the wave of nausea set in again. I don't remember too much after that, other than waking up on the bathroom floor with a blanket over me, and Christine sitting next to me, quietly stroking my hair. She kept saying, "I was really worried about you, Drew. I was really worried." I remember thinking in a real self-destructive way, if that's what it takes to get a reaction out of her, then that's what I need to do. I'm an ocean away from her now, but I can hear those words again—"I was really worried about you, Drew"— as I finally nod off.

NICK DANGER

The following Tuesday is the first day of November. On my way to a lecture I stop at the shop to buy this week's *NME* and *Melody Maker*. The Jesus and Mary Chain are on the front cover of both. Their debut album is in the shops today. I won't be going to class after all. I'll be going to Andy's Records in Colchester to buy *Psychocandy*.

On the bus ride to town I skim through the magazines. My favorite scribe, Nick Danger, reviews *Psychocandy* for *Melody Maker*. He's passionate and over-the-top as usual, telling his readers that it's Year Zero and that The Jesus and Mary Chain have drawn the line in the sand. They are the future of rock 'n' roll, he says, and if you don't like it you can fuck off and listen to Frankie Goes To Hollywood. I want to buy him a drink. Normally I like to have a bit of a walk around Colchester. It's a beautiful little town with cobblestone streets, old churches, and Roman and Medieval ruins, but today I just want to buy *Psychocandy* and get back to my room to listen to it.

It's as good as Nick says. In fact, it's the best record I've ever heard. I bought the "Never Understand," "You Trip Me Up," and "Just Like Honey" singles at Schoolkids', but it's an entirely different experience hearing those songs and eleven more as a full body of work. The album is catchy like all of the best punk pop groups, such as The Buzzcocks and Undertones, but there's so much more going on. The combination of screeching noise and heavenly melodies is intoxicating. The lyrics are dark and menacing, too. Most of the songs appear to be about girls screwing the Reid brothers over, but

Jim and William live to tell the tale, in fact they seem to relish it. "The Living End" is the perfect fuck off to everything, an *Easy Rider*-like ode to finding freedom on a motorcycle. Full of swagger Jim declares, "My mood is black when my jacket's on and I'm in love with myself... and an empty road and a cool, cool wind and it makes me feel so good." I punch the air as if I'm headbanging to Judas Priest.

"Taste of Cindy" reminds me of Christine, perhaps too much. "Knife in the back when I think of Cindy," sings Jim. "Knife in the back when I think of Christine," I sing back to Jim. "Just Like Honey" is a sober reality check. I hate how much power Christine has over me, and I hate myself for knowing that I'd probably crawl back to her if given the chance. Like that song's protagonist, I want to be her "plastic toy." I wanna be her dog.

The next day I decide to go to London and meet Nick Danger. Dave probably meant well, but it's pretty obvious that he's not going to connect me with anyone at *Melody Maker*. The last time I was in his room, I saw the copies of my press clippings in a pile with some of his class notes. Despite being in England for a full month I've only been to London once, and that was just to see an England vs. Turkey football match with some of my flatmates, piss-up beforehand on Baker Street. We didn't see Holmes and Watson.

Melody Maker is in the vicinity of Waterloo Station, just south of the Thames. I arrive at reception and nervously ask the girl behind the desk if Nick Danger is around. At first she doesn't think he is, but then an old hippie guy with a pony-tail, who looks like he could even be in his mid-thirties, says that Nick is in the back. While waiting for Nick, I'm surprised at how old some of the other people are, not just ponytail guy. In my head I somehow expected music journalists to look and dress like pop stars, resigned to a Menudo or *Logan's Run* expiration date when they got too old to be relevant. With the exception of a few trendy youngsters, who all seem to look and dress like Dave, England's tastemakers are a surprisingly bland looking bunch.

Nick isn't what I expect either. He's a few inches shorter than me, pale and thin, with messy black hair just over his ears and covering his eyes in front. He's wearing National Health specs, a thrift store cardigan over a Pastels t-shirt, brown corduroys, and Clarke's desert boots. On paper he's an angry, borderline gonzo journalist, but in person he's quiet and quite sweet.

He's flabbergasted and flattered that I've made the trip just to tell him how much I like his writing and seems genuinely interested in the press clips I hand over to him. He introduces me to his editor, who tells me in a somewhat noncommittal tone that while they're not looking for any full-time writers, they can always use live reviews from gigs in provincial outposts.

Nick asks if I have any other plans for the day. He's going back to his flat in Camden but offers to take me around to some record shops along the way. He says that Primal Scream and Meat Whiplash are playing later tonight. I haven't heard of either band, and Nick's eyes light up as he describes them.

"They're both on Creation, the label that put out the first Jesus and Mary Chain single 'Upside Down.' The label boss, Alan McGee, is a bit of a nutter but he has immaculate taste. Primal Scream is Bobby Gillespie's band. Rumor has it that he's going to quit drumming for The Jesus and Mary Chain to do it full-time, you know. He's the frontman. Not the best singer in the world but he's got a lot of soul. They're very Sixties sounding like The Byrds or Love."

Nick takes a deep breath and continues, "Meat Whiplash are from East Kilbride, Scotland. They're friends of the Reid brothers. They have a single out called 'Don't Slip Up.' It's up there with the best Mary Chain material. If you see it in a shop today, you have to buy it."

Nick's twenty-five, the same age as my brother Paul, and studied at Oxford, where he somehow managed to get an honors degree in literature while also establishing himself as an up and coming journalist. He started a fanzine at university called *Machine Gun Etiquette* (he used to be a punk he tells me with a sheepish look) and landed a job at *Melody Maker* as a result of that.

I half expect to be going on an afternoon bender—every English guy I've meet seems to be a heavy drinker—but I'm somewhat relieved to just have tea and sandwiches at a Marks and Spencer before embarking on a record shopping tour of the city.

We start at the legendary Carnaby Street. "Not at all what it used to be," says Nick, "but back in the Sixties all the mods hung out here." A few of the boutiques sell all the proper gear like Ben Sherman, Fred Perry, and Merc, but most of the stores are more or less junk shops, pedaling knockoff t-shirts of Sid Vicious and Ian Curtis. I don't see any mods. Nick tells me that the scene pretty much died as soon as The Jam broke up. I mainly see parades of goths in uniforms, consisting of black leather jackets with stenciled band logos, the most popular ones being Sisters of Mercy, New Model Army, and Gene Loves Jezebel; studded belts; and tight black jeans on the guys, leggings or long black skirts on the girls.

After Carnaby, Nick takes me to Soho where we hit some record stores on Berwick Street, the best one being Sister Ray. I buy the Meat Whiplash single and a Chameleons album, which I was never able to find in America. Once Nick gets going, he's a nonstop chatterbox, a walking music encyclopedia. He's just old enough that he was able to see all of the original punk bands in small clubs. Sex Pistols, Clash, Siouxsie and the Banshees, Gang of Four, Buzzcocks, you name it, he saw it. Why couldn't Nick be my older brother, I think for about the hundredth time that day.

Before going to the club we stop at Nick's flat, which is just a small efficiency with a tiny kitchen space. The place is covered wall to wall with records and neat stacks of music magazines. It's like a museum or a rock 'n' roll shrine, a new wave Graceland. Nick jokes, when he sees how excited I am, "Nice little collection, eh?"

"I'll say."

"To be fair, a lot of those were given to me. Journos don't make much money, but we get a lot of swag. I sometimes need to sell a few of these just to make my rent."

This surprises me. For some reason I assumed that music journalists made a decent screw. Too many Hollywood ideas in my head, I suppose.

We grab a quick pint at Nick's local before heading to the club. The venue is dank and depressing with just a small stage in back, but there's a lot of energy in the air. The place is packed, the audience consisting mainly of indie boys like Nick in cardigans or anoraks, and their female counterparts looking cute in thrift store dresses and Mary Quant or Marianne Faithfull haircuts. I suddenly feel out of place in my leather jacket until Nick introduces me to Alan McGee, who is clad head-to-toe in black leather and has a carrot orange afro, well, as much as a Scotsman can muster. His accent is indecipherable but he buys me a pint. I can understand that much, the international language of intoxication. Nick seems to know everyone and we make the rounds as Meat Whiplash begin to set up. He introduces me to the guys in Primal Scream, who will be playing after Meat Whiplash.

I'm a bit star struck when I shake Bobby Gillespie's hand. He's wearing tight black leather trousers and a floral dress shirt. I tell him how much I like *Psychocandy*, and he somewhat coldly says, "I hope you like us as much, mate." He seems to be over the Mary Chain. His shaggy haircut is really cool, pretty much what mine could be if I didn't tease it so much with spray and gel. I make a mental note to use less hair product after seeing how many cute girls come by to say hello.

Meat Whiplash blast through about a half dozen songs in fifteen minutes. They're like a Jesus and Mary Chain farm team if one were to make a baseball analogy; lots of black leather, big hair, and white noise, just not as good. It's a bit of a racket but I can hear some nice melodies buried underneath. I recognize "Don't Slip Up" (Nick played it for me at his flat) and they win further points by covering The Stooges' "I Wanna Be Your Dog."

Primal Scream is fantastic. Though I haven't heard anything by them, the songs are instantly catchy. Bobby pours his heart and soul into it and the kids are eating it up. The guitarist, Jim, is incredible. His lines are striking without succumbing to any guitar hero antics, a kindred spirit to Johnny Marr. No flash, no excess, just pure and beautiful rock 'n' roll. One song in particular floors me. Bobby tells the audience it's a new one called "Velocity Girl." It begins with the line, "Here she comes again with vodka in her veins," which is about all I manage to catch. The track is much too short, barely a minute long, ending with Bobby repeating the line, "leave me alone" over and over as the music fades out. It's timeless, melancholic and beautiful, reminiscent of my favorite Rolling Stones songs like "Paint it Black," "Heart of Stone," and "Play With Fire." Primal Scream is cut from the same cloth.

After the show ends, Nick invites me to join him for a nightcap at a Chinese Restaurant that has an afterhours liquor license.

"A bunch of us are coming. Alan and Primal Scream will be there, too."

"Shit," I say. "I'd love to, but the last train to Colchester is just after midnight. There isn't another one until like six in the morning. I should probably head back."

Nick looks at his watch and smiles, "You've already missed your train, mate. You're stuck in London until morning."

I laugh and say, "Fuck it. When in Rome."

"It'll be a laugh," Nick says. "You can crash at my place. Chances are you'll still be up at six anyway, if Alan is up to his usual tricks."

We find Alan outside the pub, directing various musicians, groupies, and assorted scenesters into a fleet of cabs that he has commandeered alongside the street. Nick and I join Alan and Bobby in the last one. It's a pretty trippy ride. Alan is in front giving the Pakistani cabby directions in his thick Scottish accent, while the equally confused cabby babbles back in indecipherable pigeon English. Nick and I can't stop laughing. Bobby, who is also Scottish, a childhood friend of Alan's from Glasgow, can't understand what's so funny.

"You lot are fookin' mental," he says.

We get to the Chinese restaurant and join about fifteen others who are sitting at three tables. I'm not that hungry but I order some Lo Mein to soak up the alcohol and wash it down with several cans of Holsten over the course of the meal. Nick and I are sitting closest to Alan and Bobby and they ask me where I'm from. I say Detroit instead of Ann Arbor, trying to put on a tough guy veneer.

"I love The MC5," says Bobby. "True revolutionaries. We cover 'Ramblin' Rose' in rehearsal now and then."

"That's really cool," I say, trying not to sound nerdy and over excited. "I imagine you like The Stooges, too."

"Of course, mate. Iggy Pop is a god," says Bobby.

He takes a sip of lager and continues, "I want the Scream to be icons like that. MC5, Rolling Stones, something larger than life. None of this poncey indie rubbish."

An equally animated, and possibly coked up, Alan adds, "That's exactly what I want Creation to be. Fookin' massive. I want all of our bands to be on *Top of the Pops*."

At this point, I have to piss pretty badly and so does Nick so we go off in search of a bathroom. We're told to go down the stairs and we can't miss it, but the stairs are dark and creaky with only a dimly lit light bulb to guide our way. I open the first door that I find, but it's just a small closet full of cleaning supplies. I start to laugh and Nick blurts out, "Hello Cleveland!"

I immediately get the *Spinal Tap* reference and laugh so hard that I almost piss myself. At this point, Bobby has joined us.

"Where's the fookin' toilet, then?" asks Bobby.

"Can't seem to find it," I say, now laughing uncontrollably.

Nick opens another door to discover another dead end—a closet full of old pots and pans.

"Hello Cleveland!" Nick screams.

Bobby immediately cottons on and he's in hysterics, too. We finally reach our destination on our third attempt, only to find the toilet and the sole urinal occupied by two of the guys from our party, with two more pissing in the sink, having a sword fight if you will. When I finally do get to piss, it feels almost orgasmic from having had to hold it so long. Weirdly, I think of Christine rather spitefully as the piss flows out of me at Space Shuttle speed. If only you could see me now, bitch, I'm living it up in the UK with the in crowd, while you're toiling away in Michigan. Fuck you.

We leave the restaurant at around 3:00am. Alan invites us to party some more at his place, but Nick and I are pretty sloshed, so we cab it back to his flat and call it a night. I immediately pass out on Nick's couch.

When I wake up at around lunch time, Nick's gone but he's left me a note with his phone number, telling me to look him up any time.

I take the Tube to Liverpool Street and sleep some more on the train to Colchester. I'm feeling wrecked, but ecstatic. I'm reinventing myself so nicely here, I think. No one needs to know that I used to be a jock until just a few years ago. No one needs to know that I got jilted by a girl that was hip by Ann Arbor standards, but couldn't hold a candle to some of the girls I saw at the show last night.

When I arrive at Eddington, I find Dave and Simon drinking tea in the common area.

"Where the fuck have you been?" asks Dave. "You look like death."

I retrace yesterday's adventures with as much embellishment as I can muster while Dave and Simon listen in disbelief. I seem to have gained some cred points from them, but also sense a little hurt and jealousy from Dave.

"So why didn't you invite me then, mate?" he asks.

I lie and tell him it was a weird spur of the moment thing, not wanting to let him know, that I knew, he hadn't passed on my writing clips to his *Melody Maker* 'connection.'

He can tell that I'm trying to be apologetic and abruptly brushes it off.

"No worries, mate. It's nothing. Nothing at all."

NAKED PUSHUPS

The following Saturday, James, my flatmate from Derby, and I decide to go out for drinks in Colchester. We try to get a full crew together, but everyone in Eddington 5 has other plans. Dave has gone home to Manchester for a long weekend. Chris is going to a Squeeze concert in Ipswich, and Alan wants to go to the disco at the basement club. We try to get another guy we know named Charles to join us. He lives in Eddington 8 and has been a tad too worked up lately—more like borderline obsessed—about a girl named Kate, who he met at a party last month. It's pretty clear that Kate isn't interested in him so a night away from the university might do him some good.

We stop at his flat on our way to town.

"We're off to Colchester, Charles. Want to join us?" asks James.

Charles is shirtless, putting on deodorant and checking himself out in the mirror. His thick brown hair has a dramatic side part and it looks like he's wearing a helmet.

"Sorry, mates. I'm going to the disco tonight with Alan. Kate might be around."

"Have you made any progress?" I ask.

"Not, really," Charles admits. "I try to talk to her, but she always brushes me off. I guess I need to be more persistent."

"Come out with us then," I say. "There are plenty of other fish in the sea."

"Yeah, there's always a pot of gold at the end of a rainbow," chimes in James.

James and I continue with this Abbot and Costello routine of clichés, which pisses off Charles to no end. He's not coming. We bus it to Colchester and go to a pub called The Castle, located around the corner from the actual castle. The building looks to have been built in the 18th Century and the décor is neo-Gothic, the kind of place Bram Stoker might have hung out at when he was writing *Dracula*.

The plan is to hang out here until closing time and then hit a nightclub called The Andromeda, which is within walking distance. I haven't gotten laid since last spring and James is in a similar slump. Easy townie girls could be the perfect tonic for our ailments.

James and I have a good chat at The Castle. We've hung out in group settings at the pub and around the flat, but never just the two of us. He's pursuing a degree in law. Unlike in the States, law is an undergraduate major in England. From what I can understand, after graduation, you get an apprenticeship with a firm and learn on the job before taking the British equivalent of the bar examination. Alan is also a law student and the two of them definitely work harder than the others in our flat, who are majoring in less challenging majors like Economics, History, and Politics.

"So what are your thoughts of England after two months here?" asks James.

"A little different than I expected. I'm definitely drinking more than I imagined." I pause to take a sip of ale. "And I'm certainly going to class less than I expected!"

"Ah, that's the way it is here. Just wait until exams; everyone will work themselves up into a frenzy. So you have another year of university?"

"Yeah, it's four years in America."

"What do you plan on doing when you finish?"

"I'm not really sure. I probably should start thinking about it. I need to write again. That's what I'm best at. Hopefully I can at least get some freelance work, even if I don't get a proper writing job."

"I saw some of your writing in Dave's room. What I

70

read was quite good."

"Thanks. Dave said he knew someone at *Melody Maker* who could help me out, but he never came through."

I try to act nonchalant, but I'm still a little ticked. "I ended up going to London and stopping by the offices myself."

"I wouldn't put too much trust in Dave. He's decent lad, but he can be a wanker."

"Like how?"

"Well, he's always had this thing for Julie, you know the girl you've been trying to get off with."

"Don't remind me. I've made less progress with her than Charles has with Kate!"

James laughs and continues, "Julie was seeing this bloke named Matthew and it was pretty serious, but even then Dave was still trying to get off with her. Matthew even confronted him once at the Union Bar. No punches were thrown but lots of shouting and shoving."

"Wow. I had no idea. He told me he had no interest in her and even introduced us."

"I'd be careful, just the same."

"Noted."

It's close to 11:00 and we head over to The Andromeda. I have a hard time keeping up. James is like 6'4" and lean and walks with a long, quick stride. I feel like I practically have to jog to keep up with him. We arrive at our destination but immediately get shot down. Turns out we have to be members to get admitted.

"How much is a membership, then?" asks James.

"Thirty quid," says the doorman.

"Thirty quid?" I inquire, not quite believing what the doorman just said.

"It's for a full year, lads. That's quite a bargain."

We decide to pass up on the marvelous opportunity.

James has another idea. "There's a club about half way between Wivenhoe and Brightlingsea. We could take a cab there. There ought to be some decent looking birds there."

"It's worth a shot. I'm game."

The cab ride is only twenty minutes but feels like an eternity. My bladder is working overtime from drinking half a dozen pints at The Castle, and as soon as we pay the entrance fee, we make a run for the toilets. At the bar, we opt for mixed drinks. Shorts as they call them here. I need to slow down on the pissing if I'm going to score. Both of us order whiskey and coke and we stroll around the noisy club, taking in the scene. The music is all very Top 40 synth pop—hell on my ears, but the punters seem to enjoy it. Groups of girls are dancing in circles, handbags placed in the middle, as if they're performing a fertility ritual around a fire. The guys hang out on the sidelines, occasionally one or two breaking off from their respective packs in a misguided attempt to penetrate a handbag circle. Some people succeed and are making out on the dance floor or in booths, but the general vibe here is one of disappointment.

We retreat to the bar and order another round, resigning ourselves to the too drunk to care zone. I start to get depressed, as I'm prone to do when I drink too much, and think about Christine. I haven't written to her since we talked on the phone last month and I wish I could just let it go. James and I were teasing Charles earlier about his obsession with Kate, but I haven't been much different with Christine. I wish I could get an in with Julie. She has that gothic beauty look I'm a sucker for, but seems to have more of a head on her shoulders than Christine. I wonder if she's at the disco. Maybe James and I should have gone there instead. It's getting close to 2:00am—closing time for nightclubs—and we decide to find a cab. There's a line of cars outside, but every single one has been reserved. This isn't good. It's about a six mile walk to campus, but we have no choice.

The cool November air feels good though and it turns out to be a nice hike. James and I amuse ourselves with some of the Eagle Scout chants that Dan taught us on the Wiv Run, and we manage to make it to Eddington by 4:00am. We decide to check up on Charles. He's up and, with the exception of a pair of skimpy bikini briefs, he's stark naked on the floor doing pushups. Not the sight we expected at all.

"Oi, Charles," says James, trying to compose himself. "What's going on, mate?"

"Working out some tension. I've already had two wanks tonight and I'm still pent up."

I start cracking up. English guys are strangely open about jerking off. Americans are much more Catholic in our attitudes. Of course we do it, but most of us deny it.

"No progress with Kate, then?" asks James.

"None at all. She torments me. I danced with her a bit and then she went off with some bloke with a flat top."

"Maybe you should get a flat top, then," teases James.

"Yeah, some of the girls here fall for that look," I say.

Sadly, it is true. There is a certain set of guys and girls here who all look and dress like they're characters in *Happy Days*, you know, checked shirts on the guys, poodle skirts for the gals.

"Think that would help me pull Kate?" asks Charles. He's being serious.

"It might not hurt," says James, holding back laughter.

"If not, there are plenty of other fish in the sea," I burst out.

"Always a pot of gold at the end of the rainbow," says James. "Take a look on the bright side of life!"

"Christ, not that again," says Charles. His face is beat red. "I'm knackered, so why don't you two piss off if you're not going to be helpful."

YOU TRIP ME UP

November is almost gone. A lot of the guys in the flat are running out of grant money for the term and there seems to be an unspoken pact amongst us that it's time to finally study. The boozing has been relegated to weekends and I've managed to finish three of my four essays, and while not great, my marks are the British equivalents of B's across the board.

I take a road trip to Norwich University to see The Jesus and Mary Chain at the end of the month with Dave, Simon, and some of the other members of the Alternative Music Society. The 'society' isn't so much a club, but rather an excuse for people to get together, talk about music, and drink copiously. We rent a van and arrive at Norwich in the early evening with just enough time to explore a little bit of the old cathedral town before darkness sets in and the pub beckons. Even though the drive is less than an hour, everything in England seems further away than it really is, mainly because every town seems to have its own distinct dialect. It's amazing how many different accents I've already encountered here, ranging from Dave's smooth Manchester lingo, to Simon's posh Queen's English, to Chris' barely decipherable Geordie speak.

Live, The Jesus and Mary Chain prove to be a bit of a disappointment, more of a circus spectacle than the amazing group that created *Psychocandy*, which I still play at least twice a day. You can tell they don't want to be there and though they look effortlessly cool in black leather, motorcycle boots, and spiky haircuts, they go through the motions. The vocals are, at times, barely audible, drowned way too low in the mix. Most of what I can hear is feedback, unbearable white noise screeching out of the massive speakers on each side of the stage. The crowd doesn't help matters. While a number of people, like our crew who made the trip from Essex, are here to see the band, others have bought into the media hype, first instigated by a riot at a Jesus and Mary Chain show in London earlier in the year. These are your typical rugby playing conservative lads who bully their way to the front of the stage and try to heckle the band.

At one point Jim tells one of them to "fook off" and threatens to bash his head with his guitar. They play twenty minutes tops and walk off to a combination of cheers and boos. Bobby looks bored. He seemed to be having much more fun at that Primal Scream show I saw with Nick. I start to think that maybe The Jesus and Mary Chain will flame out like The Sex Pistols, leaving behind just one legendary album as their legacy.

I observe all of this from the back of the crowd, where I hastily retreated after one song when it became apparent that I might lose my hearing from the feedback, or possibly get my head kicked in by a rugby lad. One of the girls from Essex named Claire has the same idea. She's the redhead who was dancing with Julie at the disco the night I did the Wiv Run. She's from Belfast and looks striking (like a sexier version of Molly Ringwald) in her black leather jacket, tight jeans, and DM boots. I ask her what Julie has been up to.

"Fancy her, eh," Claire says with a smile.

"Yeah. I do like her, but I never really see her around. I probably didn't make too great of an impression at the disco. She said something snarky to me."

"I wouldn't worry about it," says Claire. "Julie can be very serious at times. She's a lot of fun but works too hard. She's always studying."

"I doubt I'd impress her then. I haven't done too much work since I've been here."

"I know the feeling. I tend not to do anything until I

have a deadline staring me smack in the face."

"So what brought you here from Ireland?" I ask.

"I needed to get out of Belfast. Do you know much about Northern Ireland?"

"A bit. I know that most of the Catholics want to unify with the Republic and that the Unionists don't. I remember all of that stuff with Bobby Sands and the hunger strikes, too."

"Well, that's more than most people know. Anyway, I'm Protestant for what it's worth, but I don't identify with either side. I've had enough of Belfast. I'm sick of all the bloodshed. Tanks and troops in the streets, IRA bombings, Protestant retaliation shootings... I needed an escape."

She pauses before continuing. "Anyway, I wanted to go somewhere in England, London preferably, to be around a lot of live music, but I wasn't quite clever enough for that."

"You're speaking my language. I wanted to go to the LSE. Essex was my second choice."

"I think Essex is everyone's second choice."

We both laugh.

"Here's to having fun and underachieving. We may not be in London, but, hey, it's The Jesus and Mary Chain, even if they're not so good tonight," I say.

"Cheers. I'll drink to that," she says as we clink our cans of lager, while the Mary Chain muscle through "You Trip Me Up."

I'LL MELT WITH YOU

A few days later I'm in my room, working on an American History essay, the last one I need to finish for the term, when Dave stops by to tell me that Simon has gotten a hold of some hash from one of the Middle Eastern students on campus. People are in his room skinning up as we speak, he says in an animated tone. I tell him that I'll reluctantly pass, but Dave insists, adding that Robbie Grey is there.

"Who?" I ask.

"You know, Modern English. They're from Colchester you know." I didn't know that. It's just too weird of a coincidence.

Dave sings, "I'll stop the world and melt with you."

I laugh and sing back, "You've seen the difference and it's getting better all the time." I can't miss out on this.

Robbie's there with a girl who's a student at Essex and friends with Simon. Fortunately Dave doesn't introduce me as an American for once and it's a pretty chill experience as the large blunt makes its way across the room while Lloyd Cole and The Commotions' "Lost Weekend" appropriately plays in the background. Robbie and his girlfriend leave after the joint is finished and Dave, Simon, and I head over to the Union Bar laughing; so much for finishing that essay.

Later that night, I wake up from a freaky dream. I'm guessing it's the combination of Moroccan hash and multiple pints at the Union Bar, but this dream is a far out trip, one of those lucid affairs straight out of a science fiction flick.

I'm in a wide open field surrounded by Medieval Festival stalls. It must be around 1980 because The Jam are setting up, while The English Beat's version of "Tears of A Clown" plays in the background. I can see Bruce Foxton and Rick Buckler, but I can't find Paul Weller. Someone whispers that he's backstage—something about an argument with Elvis Costello about who's going to headline the bill. I'm wearing white Levi's and nothing else—barefoot in the park. Not too many people are around, just a few hippies and stoners. They're all shirtless, too, even the chicks, but it doesn't seem weird. I enter a tent where a joint is getting passed around. I take a hit. Someone asks if I'm Iggy Pop.

"No, man," I say, "I'm from the future. I'm from 1985."

A guy with flowing blonde hair, who looks like the cartoon character He-Man, has his doubts, fully convinced that I'm tripping. A beautiful brunette seems to think otherwise.

"Tell me about the future, Mr. Spaceman. Sing me a song," she asks.

I belt out the chorus of "I Melt With You" and the group nods their heads. They don't know it. I've somehow managed to crack the time and space continuum.

"That's really rad," says the brunette. "But how do I know you're really telling the truth?"

"Don't lose sight of me," I say. "I want to stay here, but I'm going to disappear soon and then you'll know I'm not lying."

"Won't you miss your home if you stay here?" she asks.

"Yes, I left the love of my life to be with you, but this experience is deeper."

I wake up, wondering who the love of my life is.

A few weeks pass, and it's now mid-December and everyone in my flat has gone home for the holidays. I've finalized plans to visit Chris in Newcastle for a week and after Christmas I'll head to Manchester to spend the last two weeks of the holiday with Dave. On the night before I depart from Essex, I have a meal at the university's Hexagon Restaurant, a large, yes, hexagon-shaped cafeteria of sorts where one pound

Sterling is enough to fill up a growing boy for hours. I select what looks like chicken and chips, and, as I pay for my meal, I notice that Julie is sitting by herself at one of the tables. I'm surprised to see her since the only students who seem to be around this late into the month are the Asians and Africans. I ask if I can join her and she says yes.

"I'm sorry about that night at the disco," I say. "I was really pissed."

"Nothing I haven't seen before. I'm English, you know." She smiles. "So what are you still doing here?"

"I'm off tomorrow to visit Chris and then Dave. What about you? Where's your family?"

"They're nearby. I'm from Chelmsford, just down the road. My mum and I aren't really getting along too well at the moment. I'll just pop over for an awkward meal at Christmas and then come back here."

"Sorry about that," I say.

"It's OK. She never liked my old boyfriend Matthew. They're from money and my family is pretty working class and my mum gave me a hard time about that. When we split up she gloated about it, which wasn't what I needed to hear."

"All this class stuff is pretty confusing. It exists in America, but it's not so in your face like it is here."

"You'll get to experience some of that this holiday," she says.

"What do you mean?"

"Well, you know, Chris is a working class lad and Dave is filthy rich."

"I didn't know that," I say, taken somewhat aback. "I thought he was totally working class. He's like the resident socialist in our flat."

"He does that for indie cred. His family is really posh. His father is some kind of banking executive in Manchester. His mate Simon was really pissed one night and told me."

After we finish eating, I ask Julie if she wants to get a drink and she says yes. We go to the Top Bar. It's cleaner than the Union Bar and while it has a more traditional pub feel, everything is very modern looking with a shiny new jukebox in the corner and a few slot machines (everyone here calls them fruit machines). If an American mall ever wanted to have a British pub on its premises, it couldn't go wrong with the Top Bar as a template.

Julie orders a glass of wine and I have a pint.

"So where are you from?" she asks.

"Michigan."

"What's it like there?"

"It's too cold in the winter and too hot in the summer. I'm not far away from Detroit. It used to be a big automobile town but now it's pretty crime-ridden."

"So what are your plans when you finish your degree?"

"I really have no idea. I have one more year of university when I get home, but I'm pretty clueless. To be honest I don't even want to think about going home. I wish I could just stay here. I want to be a writer. I just met Nick Danger from *Melody Maker* and I might be able to write some reviews for them."

"That sounds promising," she says, but her tone seems more matter of fact than utterly thrilled. "I used to always read *Melody Maker* and *NME*, not so much anymore. Matthew wanted to be involved with music. He was in the Entertainment Society here, but now he's working for the Bank of England."

"That doesn't sound like fun. What about you? What do you want to do?"

Julie takes a sip of wine and says, "I'm doing a degree in literature and I've been offered a spot to stay here and pursue an M.A., but I'm not sure if I want to be in Colchester for another year. It's a good opportunity though and it could lead to a teaching position."

We have a few more drinks and I can tell she's getting a little lightheaded. I feel like I'm just warming up; the two and a half months here has boosted my tolerance to ridiculous levels. I try to get a read on Julie. She's not conservative, at least not in a political sense, but she's definitely not a partier. Her long, straight black hair and fashionable black dress give her a timeless English look, not unlike the retro Sixties girls I saw at the Primal Scream show. She tells me that her favorite bands are The Smiths, Aztec Camera, and The Undertones, but that she doesn't really like going to concerts anymore and doesn't really follow the music scene much, preferring to read Jane Austen and Thomas Hardy instead.

While we're the same age, she seems to be a lot more grown up than I am, though she does laugh when I call her Julie Ocean after she mentions The Undertones. At least she has a sense of humor. When the pub closes I walk her home, well, walk her to where she's staying. Julie rents a room in Colchester, but is staying at Claire's room in Bertrand Russell Tower—which is situated right next to Eddington—while Claire is off visiting her family in Belfast. Just as we're about to say goodbye, Julie asks if I would like to come in for a cup of tea; a good sign.

The layout of Bertrand Russell 7 is identical to Eddington 5 though much cleaner since the tenants are all girls. The guys in my flat are so messy that the cleaning ladies on occasion will refuse to pick up until we make things borderline acceptable. Sometimes it feels like I'm living with the Young Ones.

Julie gets the kettle going and breaks out a packet of McVitie's biscuits. Like most Brits, she has a sweet tooth. She brings me a cup, sits next to me on the sofa, and for the next few hours, and, a few more rounds of tea, we have a good chat. She was born in Brixton, a not so nice neighborhood in London that I only know from The Clash song "Guns of Brixton." When she was twelve she and her family were able to get a council house in Chelmsford. I learn that her dad is a long distance truck driver and her mom and younger sister work in the same factory. Julie is the only person in her family who has ever gone to a university and now it looks like she'll be the only one to pursue a graduate degree.

I tell her about my family and how I'm the odd one

out because of my average grades, above average athletic talents, and an overzealous interest in rock 'n' roll. I tell her that I'll probably be the only one in my family to not get a graduate degree.

Julie asks about my personal life and if I have a girlfriend at home. I pause and try to keep things as simple as possible, as I wash down half a biscuit with a mouthful of tea.

"I had a girlfriend for about four or five months, but that was a year ago. There hasn't been anyone since then," I say, trying to be as nonchalant as possible. The last thing I'd want Julie to know was how much I still jerked off thinking about Christine.

"Why did you split up?"

"To be honest, I wanted more out of it than she did. I think for a brief moment I was really ready to settle down, even though I was only like nineteen at the time; silly as that sounds."

"I was all ready to marry Matthew and even leave university early for him," she responds. "Matthew kept talking about getting engaged when he finished his degree, but when he did, he got cold feet and moved to London."

"That's too bad. I mean it is if you still miss him."

"I don't any more. I feel ready to move on, but I don't want a fling. Your mate Dave is always trying to get into my knickers. I don't need any of that."

I'm starting to discover that my 'mate' Dave is full of surprises. I don't mind that he's wealthy (half of my friends in Ann Arbor are quite well off), but James warned me that he could be a bit of a wanker, and now I get confirmation that he's still been chasing Julie. I wonder what this could lead to if I make any headway with her. Will it mess up our friendship?

"No comment," I say.

"What do you mean?" she asks, somewhat perplexed.

I fill her in and tell her the story of how I asked Dave to introduce the two of us. "I kind of mucked that up a bit," I say.

"Well I invited you up just now, didn't I?"

"So does that mean I have a chance?"

"It does if you're honest with me. I hate it when people lie to me. Matthew was always saying he was going to the library when he was really going to the pub. My dad's like that with my mum too. Why do men have such a hard time with the truth?"

"I'm no philosopher."

"Well, you're pretty charming for an American," she says, putting emphasis on the word American to make fun of Dave.

I laugh and she kisses me. I kiss her back, but can tell that she's not going to let me go beyond that. When I finally leave for the evening she says, "Look me up when you get back." I say I will.

HIT THE NORTH

The next day I check my mail before flagging a cab to the Colchester train station. It's been about a week since I last checked my box and I have three letters. One is from my parents; another from my brother, a total surprise (the two of us almost never communicate); and the third is from Christine. I open my parents' letter first, just a quick note to say hello and a much-needed check. Paul says something about being in London for a few days in March for an academic conference and maybe we could meet up? I'll deal with that later. Christine sends me a Christmas card. When I open it, there's a glossy black and white photo of her inside. It's pretty professional, which makes me immediately suspicious of what she might be up to, but it's so sexy that I can't help but be aroused. She's wearing a microscopic black leather skirt, fishnets, dominatrix boots, and a tight sleeveless top, tits practically exploding out. She's also brandishing a whip. The note on the card simply says, "Merry Christmas! Hope you haven't been too bad this year or I might have to punish you. Love, Christine."

I arrive in Newcastle in the early evening, lightly buzzed from the three cans of lager I had on the train, and worked up over the hot photo of Christine. I scarf down a nice traditional home cooked meal with Chris' family—meat, potatoes, and mushy peas. I can't remember the last time I had anything that wasn't of the bland cafeteria variety from the Hex, a meat pie from the Union Bar, or something hastily thrown together in the flat like Heinz baked beans on toast. Chris' family lives in a small village about fifteen minutes from the city and he takes me on a stroll through town, hitting five or six pubs with some of his Northern mates, who join us for the crawl. When the pubs close we go to an Indian restaurant with an afterhours license and I wash down a mild curry with several Castelmaine XXXX lagers. The guys, all veterans of English piss-ups, tease me for getting the curry, instead of the lethally spicy vindaloos they select.

My Newcastle routine is pretty much the same. Sleep in, eat, listen to music on Chris' stereo while reading music magazines, eat again, go to the pub, repeat. We do see a Newcastle versus Liverpool football match to break up the monotony, and the atmosphere is pretty thrilling and scary. We stand on the Newcastle side and our section is so tightly packed that at times I feel like I'm really going to get crushed. The fans are much more vocal than Americans at baseball or football games, constantly singing and chanting. As we leave the ground, we watch armored policemen escort the Liverpool fans to their buses, while a Newcastle mob mercilessly taunts them.

On Christmas Eve Chris and I cab it to the city center with a few of his mates. One of them is especially drunk and programs a jukebox to play Bruce Springsteen's version of "Santa Claus is Coming to Town" four times in a row. Some of the punters get annoyed and throw us dirty looks, so we move on to a new pub, which is playing a bunch of oldies. We end the night with everyone at the table singing Dylan's "Mr. Tambourine Man," purposely over-enunciating Bob's nasal tone.

While Newcastle was good clean PG fun, Manchester turns out to be more of the R and X rated variety. Dave is indeed as wealthy as Julie led me to believe. His family lives in a posh village called Alderley Edge, about ten miles south of Manchester. My first impression of the municipality is that the architecture and layout of Alderley High Street seems very much like Colchester or any of the other smaller towns I've stumbled across on my journey thus far, but on closer inspection, I notice pricey restaurants in lieu of chip shops, high end boutiques in place of bargain stores, wine bars where pubs ought to be. It's one of those kind of places.

Dave's family lives in a massive Tudor style house with a large garden, somewhat isolated from their neighbors. It was constructed to look old, but I can tell that it was built fairly recently. The interior décor is immaculate; expensive couches, tables, and chairs that look freshly delivered from an award winning showroom. Original art adorns the walls in almost every room, most likely selected to match the furniture rather than any aesthetic reason. I notice a couple of photos of Dave on the mantel where he's posing in boxing gear, fists up in a proper prizefighter pose. He looks to be about fourteen.

His parents, who appear to be in their late forties, look and act like they're paid spokespeople for Thatcher's England, a government that has benefitted the few at the expense of the vast majority. I can immediately see where Dave's rebellious socialist streak comes from. His folks seem really impressed that I'm American and they bombard me with tales of travel to San Francisco, Los Angeles, New York, and Disney World when Dave was a kid. I don't have the heart to tell them I've never been to any of those places. They ask me about my family and seem to like the fact that my parents are academics and that my brother is upwardly mobile, too. When I say that I want to be a rock journalist, Dave's dad looks aghast as if I had admitted that I was a pedophile, before snidely remarking, "I can see why you and our Dave are mates. I don't understand why you lot like to slum it so much. Dave wants to work for a bloody record label. We'll have to get him sorted out when he gets his degree."

Dave and I escape to a village pub as soon as possible. His first words after settling into his pint are, "Bloody hell. That's why I try not to tell people where I'm from. They'll immediately assume I'm a posh wanker."

"I know the feeling. You've heard me rant about my brother enough."

"Thank fucking god I don't have any siblings," Dave says. "My parents are bad enough."

We spend the evening getting pissed and bitching

about our families and on the way home we stop at a park bench and smoke a joint, probably the biggest act of defiance that has ever been perpetrated in this Stepford-like hamlet.

I ask about the photos on the mantel.

"I was an amateur boxer when I was a lad," says Dave.

"I used to run cross country and track and field—what you call athletics over here."

"Funny how sport can mean so much to you and then you just stop," says Dave.

"So when was the last time you fought?"

"Officially or unofficially?" he asks with a chuckle.

"Ha! I guess both."

"I stopped boxing when I was sixteen, but I've been in a few football related scuffles since then. I know some lads who are avid Manchester United supporters and I've been in street fights with opposition crews."

"Wow," I say. "Well I'm glad we're friends. I might need your back some day."

"That you have. We're thick as thieves, mate."

New Year's Eve is pretty mellow, just a night of drinking in a local pub, but a few days later we go to a warehouse party, hosted at a railway arch near Piccadilly Station. Some enterprising DJ rented it from British Rail for the evening under the guise that it was for a movie shoot. We're with one of Dave's mates, Will, who attends Manchester University. There's a really good band playing that evening called The Stone Roses, he says. He tells us that they played at his university in November and while their single is "quite goth," they have more of a rock 'n' roll vibe live. "If you like The Chameleons, you'll like The Stone Roses," he says.

On the cab journey to the city he tells me about another new Manchester combo called The Happy Mondays, who are really hard. I ask him what he means by hard and Will responds, "You know, hard men. They're bloody criminals and drug dealers, who somehow got signed to Factory Records. I think Tony Wilson might be losing the plot. They're a scary bunch."

The warehouse is packed when we get there. We've had a few pints in the village but need to feed our appetite some more. We find someone selling overpriced cans of lager from a cooler. That'll do for now. The crowd is quite eclectic, a combination of indie kids, mean looking men in tracksuits and trainers, and, even, some borderline hippies. A lot of the girls and a few of the guys are wearing flared jeans, just like the kind I wore in grade school.

"I wish I had some cannabis," says Dave. "I wouldn't mind pulling one of those hippie birds."

"Someone is bound to have some," says Will. "Let's try to work our magic."

The DJ is playing dance music that is unlike anything I've ever heard. The sound is beat heavy but nothing remotely like disco; this is much more minimalist and futuristic. It almost feels like the Terminator could make a guest appearance, but, fortunately, the vibes here are too peaceful to warrant a visit from Arnold. I immediately want to be on whatever they're on. We work our way closer to the front where the band is setting up. The guy I presume to be the singer is wearing skinny jeans with a paisley shirt, hair slicked back. Next to him is a guy holding a paint-splashed guitar that looks like a Jackson Pollack creation. He has a shaggy haircut, just like Bobby Gillespie, and is wearing a paisley shirt with faded flared black jeans.

We see three girls dancing together and they look ecstatic. One of them runs over to Will and runs her fingers through his thick brown hair. "Your hair feels so nice," she keeps saying. She leads him away. Dave and I look at each other in bewilderment.

The other two remain with us. One is tall and thin with a short brown bobbed haircut. She looks pretty young, maybe seventeen or eighteen. I hope she's not younger than that. She's wearing bell-bottom jeans over a pair of red and white adidas gazelles and a Manchester United jersey. Her friend is shorter, a little on the chubby side, and very well endowed. She's wearing a skirt and heels, more of soul girl. I ask them if they have anything to smoke, adding that the lagers aren't really cutting it. Man Utd girl hands me a pill.

"What's this?" I ask.

"Just take it. Trust me," she says with a cute smile.

I wash it down with the last of my lager.

"Oi, you got one for me?" asks Dave.

"I can get you one," says the chubby girl as she takes Dave's hand and leads him away.

"Let's dance," says Man Utd girl.

I feel a little awkward at first as I try to go with the flow before realizing that no one here gives a shit. They're just having a good time. No judge, jury, or dance floor executioner. I'm buzzed from the lager and watching Man Utd girl glow. She seems almost angelic. The band begins to play and they're great. The sound is heavy at times, but the guitarist is a maestro, conjuring up all kinds of cool effects like The Edge or Reg and Dave from The Chameleons. A few songs in and I'm suddenly feeling happier than I've ever been in my whole life. Everything is so beautiful. I kiss her and she kisses me back. The singer is singing something about wanting to be adored and I couldn't say it better myself.

Man Utd girl is rubbing my crotch while my right hand is working its way underneath her jersey. She isn't wearing a bra. We go over to an isolated section of the warehouse and notice other couples going at it. Was Woodstock like this? I think I see Dave and his new friend but I'm not too sure. God knows where Will is. I laugh at the memory of that girl running her fingers through his hair. What the hell am I on? I feel like the world is moving in slow motion as Man Utd girl unzips my jeans and places her hand inside my boxers. I return the favor and run my hand over her panties before she guides my fingers underneath, whispering, "That's perfect. Don't stop." I'm pretty close to climaxing and the sensations feel incredible. Afterward we laugh like school kids and kiss some more.

When the gig ends, we manage to find Dave and chubby and a few minutes later, Will. Will doesn't know where his friend wandered off to. She seemed to lose interest, he says. "That bird was higher than the bloody sun."

The four of us giggle.

"Should have popped a magic bean," says Dave.

Will doesn't know what the fuck we're talking about.

"We better find her," says Man Utd girl. We say good-bye and French kiss one last time. Dave and chubby do the same and Will turns away in mock disgust.

"Fookin' hell," he mumbles.

When the girls leave, the three of us wander off in search of a cab. Rather, Will is doing the work. Dave and I are as high as the Hindenburg and completely useless. The three of us come across a doner kebab stand and I'm suddenly hypnotized as I gaze at the revolving lamb carcass getting sliced into sandwich meat by the sharp butcher's knife. Dave says something about this tasting better than the last supper as we scarf down our meals.

"She was a fookin' dirty bird," says Dave. "I shagged her in the alley, proper doggy style. How about you mate?" he asks.

"I don't kiss and tell, but I did get my rocks off, so to speak."

"Fookin' wankers," says Will. "I ended up just watching the bloody band and buying more lager."

He excuses himself to piss in an alley before we soldier on in our eternal quest for a taxi. We eventually make it to Dave's house in the wee hours of the morning and I pass out in the guest room stinking of sex, sweat, and kebab grease.

If the Stone Roses was the Woodstock moment of my trip, The Hacienda, a few nights later, was most definitely Altamont.

Dave and I meet up with an older friend of his, who now has a flat in the city. He's some kind of account executive. A real social climber, says Dave. "Brendan can be a bit of a wanker," he warns, "but he's always good for a laugh."

Dave and I go to a pub for a few hours before arriving at Brendan's flat. While small, it has all mod cons; lots of shiny chrome, an expensive hi-fi and telly, and a well stocked bar. Brendan is short, loud, and cocky; a British yuppie, who probably votes Tory. He's wearing designer jeans, a silky dress shirt, and a padded gray blazer.

Dave compliments the flat. He hasn't seen it before.

"Bloody right," says Brendan. "It's a den of seduction. Birds are always coming and going. Usually coming," he adds with emphasis.

"I've got something you might like," he says looking straight at me.

He takes out some cocaine and draws three neat lines on the glass coffee table.

"You probably do this all the time," he says.

"Actually, just once."

"Really?"

He seems surprised. I'm not that eager to get coked up, but I don't want to spoil the fun for those two... when in Rome.

"I thought Americans did blow like it was coffee. You know, *Miami Vice*, *Scarface*…" It sounds really funny hearing a British guy say blow.

"You see too many movies, Brendan," I say.

We all laugh and then do our lines before driving to the Hacienda.

Manchester looks a lot like Detroit at night, an industrial revolution wonder city that has now seen better days. I was always scared when PJ and I drove to Detroit; a lot of the neighborhoods there had non-functioning street lamps and the two of us would always run red lights, too scared to stop and risk getting jacked. Manchester isn't that bad, but we drive past a few sections that I would definitely avoid, even in daytime. New Order is appropriately enough pumping on the stereo (The Hacienda is their club after all)—*Power, Corruption & Lies*. "5 8 6" kicks in, Barney prophesying, "I see danger, danger, danger..."

The Hacienda is a downer. While the venue itself is breathtaking with its high, cathedral-like ceiling and ultra-modern veneer, the vibe is all wrong. I love Joy Division and New Order, but tonight it's just a dance DJ and I'm not feeling it. It's a posh crowd in designer clobber and I look glaringly out of place in a t-shirt, jeans, and leather jacket. I'm surprised they even let me and Dave in. They must have liked Brendan's blazer.

I sit at the bar, nursing a Stella, watching Dave and Brendan make idiots of themselves on the crowded dance floor. At one point Brendan gets into a scuffle with this tall skinny guy, who is dancing with a weird robot like motion. His moves are a combination of Ian Curtis and John Travolta if that even seems conceivable. He seems pretty smashed, not someone you'd want to mess with. Dave breaks it up and Brendan heads off to the bathroom in a huff. I notice that Mr. Roboto follows him and I race off to notify Dave.

"Fucking hell, this isn't good," he says.

We run to the bathroom just in time to witness Brendan taking a punch to the gut. Brendan tries to get away but Mr. Roboto has him in a headlock. Dave jumps in and pushes Mr. Roboto away. Mr. Roboto pushes Dave back and Dave punches him solidly in the nose. I hear a crunch and watch blood gush out of Mr. Roboto's nose like a stream from a fountain. Brendan looks aghast and I imagine I must, too. Dave continues to beat the crap out of this guy. He has him down on the ground rolling in agony while repeatedly striking him in the face. I suddenly remember the boxing photos on his parents' mantel.

"We better get out of here," I finally manage to gasp.

I'm worried that Mr. Roboto has friends at the club and I'm in no mood to get my ass kicked by Manchester toughs. Brendan doesn't look like much of a fighter either.

"Yeah, we better leave," agrees Brendan.

It's raining and the three of us are running as fast as we can in the direction of Brendan's car. "I see danger, danger, danger…" A few blocks later we stop to catch our breath, hands on our knees.

"Christ, what the fuck just happened?" I ask. I'm

really freaked out. I've witnessed fights before but nothing this vivid.

"Not sure," Dave replies in a distant tone. "I was just looking out for my mate. Are you alright, Brendan?"

"Oi, I'm OK. That bloody wanker came at me out of nowhere. You really saved my arse, Dave. I think you broke his nose."

I feel sick to the stomach at the thought and start to dry heave.

"Alright there, mate?" asks Dave, putting his hand on my shoulder.

"Yeah, I'm OK; too much lager and too much running."

Brendan has a black eye, but is otherwise unscathed. We go back to his place and sip scotch while he ices his eye. He eventually passes out and Dave looks over to me.

"I hope I didn't scare you. I got carried away a bit. It must have been the cocaine. I felt like a god. I would have done the same for you. You're a good mate, Drew."

"Likewise," I say, feeling uneasy. Only a few days ago I joked about Dave's fighting prowess, but after witnessing so much violence firsthand, it doesn't seem so funny.

THE BOY LOOKED AT JOHNNY FROM NYU

It's early January and I'm thankful to be back at Essex. I feel like I've aged five years in the two weeks I spent in Manchester. Dave must feel the same way. The two of us barely speak on the train to London, lost in our Walkmen and magazines. We're too listless to even buy cans of lager. That fight at the Hacienda freaked me out. I wonder what Dave thinks.

When we change trains at Liverpool Street Station and head to Colchester, I start to feel normal again. I try to psychoanalyze my fall from grace. Hooking up with Man Utd girl was fun at the time but Christ, I feel gross now. I think about Julie and realize that I hadn't thought of her much while I was away. The possibility of a safe, secure relationship feels really good right now. Even though Julie and I only kissed, it felt like there was potential for more, but the ball is clearly in my court.

I sent Christine a quick postcard from Manchester thanking her for the card and photo, which I admit I pulled out a few times on the trip as a performance aid. Is it even worth pursuing anything with Julie when I'm going home in June? The thought of Christine always makes me harder than a Seventies porn star on Spanish Fly, but when I really think about it, the cold truth is that the sex was the best thing. At times she could be sweet, like in tender moments when we'd sip wine and listen to music, but we never really had real conversations, certainly nothing deeper than chats about music and fashion. Christine's a stone fox, but how long can I ride out a life of sex, drugs, and rock 'n' roll? After all, I turn twenty-one next week.

I get depressed thinking about going back to Ann Arbor. God knows what I'll do when I graduate. Maybe I should look into finishing school here. A picture enters my head of living in some nice little flat in Colchester with Julie, taking walks on the cobblestone streets, checking out the castle and the Roman ruins. She'll be able to finish her masters and I'll get my degree. After that, we could move to London, where she could get a teaching job. But what would I do? Nick's a big time writer and he barely scrapes a living off *Melody Maker*. I feel doomed and destined to return to America.

We get to Eddington in the late afternoon and I take a long shower, turning the heat up as high as it can go, trying to cleanse myself from the seedy trip up North. I decide to shave, even though I kind of like the three-day stubble look. I put on some clean jeans and a black dress shirt, grab my leather jacket and pop around to Claire's room to see if Julie's still around.

Claire says Julie is back in Colchester. She invites me in and we have a quick chat while she rummages through her address book for Julie's info. Claire has some cool posters on her wall, including The Jesus and Mary Chain, Sisters of Mercy, and Psychedelic Furs. Seeing how well her tastes match up with mine, I tell her about The Stone Roses gig in Manchester. She tells me about a fun New Year's party she went to in Belfast that had a really good DJ. Finally, she writes down Julie's phone number on a small piece of pink notebook paper.

"Julie's talked quite a bit about you."

"Nothing too bad, I hope."

"Not yet," she responds with a teasing smile.

I call Julie. It seems to be a communal phone. The guy who answers says he'll see if she's around and about a minute later Julie is on the horn. She asks when I got back and I say just a few hours ago.

"Nice of you to call so soon then," she says.

She invites me over. She lives with three other students in a detached house in Colchester, about half way between the

University and the city center, a twenty-five minute walk that seems to be entirely uphill. At least the walk back should be easy. Her room is neat and clean. Clothes ironed and hung in the closest, books lined up perfectly on the shelves, probably in alphabetical order for all that I know. She has some tasteful art prints on her walls (mainly French stuff from what I can tell), along with a Smiths *Hatful Of Hollow* poster, the only homage to rock 'n' roll. There's a little red portable turntable on the floor with a stack of 45's nearby.

"Cool collection," I say as I thumb through singles by Siouxsie and The Banshees, The Smiths, Aztec Camera, Depeche Mode, Echo and The Bunnymen, and U2.

"I like singles," she says. "The artwork is always better. I used to buy a couple of 45's every week when I was in Sixth Form."

I ask if she's eaten yet. She hasn't. She says she needs to stop by the university to get a book from the library, so we head back to Essex.

"Feel like going to the Hex, then? My treat," I say.

"The Hex? Why how romantic of you. Sure." She's in a good mood.

When we go outside she takes my hand. I'm a little surprised.

"Don't be so nervous," she says.

"I'm not. I just wasn't sure that you liked me."

"I decided I do."

"So when did you decide that?" I ask as I laugh.

"Just now."

She asks me about Newcastle and Manchester and I give her a PG13 version of my escapades. No need to bring up awkward Sid and Nancy-style back alley sex or Hacienda punch ups. At the Hex I opt for fish and chips while Julie gets vegetarian lasagna. I see Dan from the flat with some of the other Americans and wave. They're sitting nearby, so we stop to say hi and I introduce Julie to the crew. There's a guy I don't know sitting at their table. He's wearing a black Fred Perry shirt with red and white trim and has neatly cropped dark brown hair just like Paul Weller or Pete Townshend circa 1965.

Dan introduces us. "Drew, this is Johnny. He just got here from NYU. He's really into music like you are. I'm sure you'll get along famously."

Wow, an American mod. Nice! I suddenly don't feel like the only weird Yank on campus. I ask Johnny if he's going to see Easterhouse on Wednesday night and he says he is.

"Let's have a pint beforehand if you're up for it."

"Sure," he says.

We agree to meet up at The Union Bar before the show.

Julie and I find a table and she teases me, "If I didn't know any better I'd think you were more enamored with Johnny than you are with me. He's very cute," she adds.

"He seems really cool. First American I've met here other than Dan who isn't so damn normal."

I see Julie every day that week. She studies a lot, so usually it's just at dinnertime when we go to the Hex or when we hang out in my room, quietly playing cassettes while we study and take breaks to make out. I've made an effort to get the room into order and it looks really good. The walls are covered with posters. Two of them I brought from home; the famous *London Calling* cover shot of Paul Simonon smashing his bass guitar and another one of the Psychedelic Furs' first LP cover. The others I recently purchased from a guy who was selling posters and bootleg cassettes one night in front of the Union Bar; the same *Psychocandy* one that Claire has in her room and another one of Echo and The Bunnymen's *Songs To Learn And Sing*, where the band is walking in single file, black and white silhouettes contrasting with a cloudy, mustard yellow background.

Julie finds my flatmates to be a little on the noisy side, but tries to limit her visits from Colchester to the university, so she spends more and more time at my 'pad.' At first I was nervous about having Julie over so often because I've seen how bad the guys can get—last term one of my flatmates, Craig, a lad from Portsmouth brought home a girl and someone came up with the bright idea of leaving a bowl outside his door to signify that he picked up a dog! She was livid though he thought it was kind of funny. I seem to be off the hook as it's a new term and everyone is flushed with grant money again, too busy frequenting the pub to have time for misogynistic mischief.

I meet up with Johnny at the Union Bar on Wednesday. I invite along Dave, but he and Simon are officers in the Entertainment Society and they're having dinner with Easterhouse before the gig—a tough job. Johnny is wearing a black suit with a black and white checked Ben Sherman shirt and looks incredibly sharp. I feel like a slob in comparison in jeans, new Jesus and Mary Chain t-shirt I bought in Manchester and my leather jacket.

We have a few pints and I learn that Johnny is a guitarist, whose band Competition Orange (named after a race car color) has actually put out a 45 called "Amphetamine Girl." He says he has a few extra copies and will give me one. I mention that I'm a writer and tell him about my articles for *The Daily* and the day I spent with Nick Danger in London. The two of us are chattering like speed freaks who've known each other forever. I get him up to snuff about Essex and tell him all the highs and lows of my first term. It feels like I've gone through a lifetime here, but it's only been about three months since I flew into Heathrow with the Thompson Twins from Iowa.

Johnny asks me about Julie and I tell him that we only met at the end of the last term, so it's still very early. He says he doesn't have a girlfriend in New York, but mentions an Italian chick named Sophia who he met in Spain last summer. He's hoping to visit Italy over spring break to see her and asks if I might want to join him. I tell him that sounds fantastic. I get the feeling that Johnny can pick up women with a snap of his fingers, but he seems pretty smitten with Sophia.

We get to the basement club just as Easterhouse are ready to go on. The place is only half full since it's mid-week and Easterhouse aren't too established. We buy cans of lager and I notice Dave and Simon and nod to them. I introduce Johnny, but it's too noisy to have any real conversation. I sense that Dave doesn't like it that Julie and I are hanging out, something I suspected might happen after Julie and James filled me in on the back story. Perhaps I'm imaging things, but Dave and I haven't talked much since Manchester. That can't be denied.

Easterhouse are amazing. They've warmed up for The Smiths in the past and tonight they're really tight. They blow away the maybe one hundred people who were smart enough to attend. They're fronted by a soulful vocalist named Andy Perry. His brother Ivor plays lead guitar and he's the second maestro I've seen in the past month (I've since learned that The Stone Roses' axe man is named John Squire). Easterhouse play their fantastic Rough Trade single "Whistling In The Dark" early on and it's just as potent live, a cross between The Smiths and The Chameleons with a little bit of early U2 in the mix. From what I've read about the group, I know that they're hardcore socialists and on stage Andy rants about various political injustices in between songs. From what I can gather he's pro-IRA, is disgusted by the British Labour Party for being sellouts, hates Thatcher (no surprise there) and admires Lenin. They have a slow burning ballad called "Lenin in Zurich" that captivates me, as does another song, a rocker called "Get Back To Russia."

After the gig as we're walking up the stairs to the main campus square, Johnny asks about *Psychocandy*. He's heard "Never Understand" and "Just Like Honey," but nothing more—the album isn't even out in America yet. I tell him that I have more than half of a bottle of Jack Daniels in my room if he wants to hang out. He's game. I feel like I'm making more of an effort to impress Johnny than Julie, but he already feels like the brother or best friend I've always wished for.

I play Johnny *Psychocandy* and a few other things and we get pretty polluted on bourbon. He tells me about his

102

band. Most of them are still in school, but they want to make a go of it after they graduate. They put out their seven-inch on a small indie label but Johnny says that Caroline Records has expressed interest in a full-length. He adds that the other guys in the group are mad that he's gone to England on "sabbatical" as he describes it, but says that he couldn't pass up the opportunity. Johnny knows all the classic mod, ska, and 2-Tone records and says he'll play me some stuff when I tell him that my knowledge of those genres is pretty limited.

"You really need to hear The Creation and The Small Faces, man," he says betraying a New York accent with his passion. He asks me to take him to London soon and I say "anytime, man." We're drunk and the 'mans' are flying back and forth. I haven't shot the shit with an American in a long time and it almost feels like I'm a drug addict that's jumped off the wagon.

The next morning, hung over as hell, I type up a review of the Easterhouse concert on my flatmate Alan's typewriter and mail it to Nick Danger, just catching the early post.

I turn twenty-one on Friday and Julie takes me out to dinner in Colchester to celebrate. We're supposed to meet up with Dave and Simon and some of the other guys later at the Union Bar, but I want to get some quiet time first. She spent the night in my room on Thursday and though we didn't have intercourse, we got as far as I did with Man Utd girl in Manchester. Julie mentions something about it being weird to have an American boyfriend and that seems to cement the deal that I'm now in a relationship.

We go to a place called Pizza Land in Colchester, which is like an upscale version of Pizza Hut. Not that the British can really make great Italian food, but it's not a bad atmosphere. We order a bottle of wine and I actually feel grown up for a change. Turning twenty-one in England seems a little melodramatic since the drinking age here is only eighteen. Julie is pretty tipsy since she's not a heavy drinker and when we get to the bus stop, we start to make out while waiting for our ride. The evening is looking promising.

We meet Dave and Simon and the rest of the crew at the Union Bar and they all buy me drinks. I try to pace myself best as I can. Julie stopped drinking for the evening and I'm scared to ruin things if I get too drunk. A flashback of the Wiv Run enters my head when I made an ass of myself in front of her. My friends all want to go to the afterhours disco in the basement, but Julie and I decide to call it a night.

"You're disappointing me, old man," says Dave in a slightly spiteful tone.

"Another time," I say.

We go back to Eddington and start to make out on my bed before Julie stops me and says she wants to take a shower. I join her and we start to go at it again, the combination of her handiwork and hot water gets me hard and raging to go. She asks if I have a Johnny (Brit slang for a condom). I never bothered to wear them when I was with Christine because she was on the pill, maybe not the best idea in retrospect, but fortunately I have a pack that has been gathering dust on my dresser. Julie seems a little more uptight in the bedroom than Christine, who was always horny and never required too much foreplay. It takes a while to get her off and for once I'm thankful to be wearing a condom to numb the sensations and prevent me from getting my rocks off too soon.

She's pretty emotional afterward, and, as we lie in bed, she starts to cry. I freak out. "Did I do something wrong?" I ask. Christ.

"No," she says. "It's just that I haven't been with anyone since I split up with Matthew last June. It feels really nice."

"It's been about a year for me, too," I lie. She doesn't need to know about any of the one-night stands I had post-Christine, like Ali or deadhead Sunshine, certainly not Man Utd girl.

Holding each other tightly, she says she loves me. Without really thinking things through, I say I love her, too.

ENGLISH ROSE

One of Julie's favorite records is The Jam's posthumous compilation album called *Snap!* Her favorite song on there is a ballad called "English Rose," so I start to call her my English Rose. I'm not used to being open and affectionate. No one ever really shared his or her feelings in my family, so I grew up tending to keep my thoughts to myself. Julie is all about being open and honest. Sometimes it feels like she's prying, as if she's trying to catch me off guard. Maybe it's the guilt I have about not being completely clean about my past.

Julie's told me all about her up and down two-year relationship with Matthew. They met on her first night at Essex at a disco. She says Dave was with Matthew that night and the two of them both wanted to pull her. Matthew apparently won out because he let Dave have a go at someone else a previous time and the rest was history, a very rocky history. She says they either got on really well or constantly fought. She visited his family for a week in Hampshire and said it was awful and that his parents hated her. I don't say anything, wondering what she might think of mine.

The only time I've argued with Julie was when I caught her going through my desk, looking at my portfolio of articles that were published in *The Daily*, the same ones I gave to Nick Danger.

"What are you doing?" I asked. "Those are private."

"You should be able to share anything with me."

"I'm not hiding anything. Just ask first."

She's visibly upset and apologizes. "Those articles are really good by the way."

I say I'm sorry and we make up. I realize that while Julie says all the things to me that I wished Christine would have said—like "I love you" a lot—I'm constantly on pins and needles with her. She's so much more sensitive than Christine.

The Tuesday after the Easterhouse show I go to the university shop for my weekly *NME* and *Melody Maker* fix and nearly have a heart attack. *Melody Maker* has published a condensed version of my review! My flatmates are all really impressed. Even Dave who's been hard to read lately says, "Fookin' *Melody Maker*. Well done, mate." Johnny and I skip class for celebratory pints at the Union Bar.

Buzzed from our lunchtime libations, I phone Nick and thank him profusely. He says that they were planning to run a review of the Easterhouse show at Kent University the previous evening, but the guy who was supposed to write the article flaked out on them. Talk about being in the right place at the right time. Nick says they can't pay me officially as I'm an American working under the table, but invites me to come down to the office and says he'll sort me out with some swag and buy me a pint.

The next day I take Johnny to London to meet up with Nick at the *Melody Maker* offices. Nick and Johnny immediately bond as they geek out on all things mod and 2-Tone, raving about The Jam, The Chords, Secret Affair, The Specials, and The English Beat, plus a bunch of groups I've never heard about. Nick lets me grab some promo cassettes. On a whim I select a copy of the latest Hüsker Dü album, *Flip Your Wig*, which Johnny says I'll love. He says it's poppier than their earlier work without losing any of the intensity. Johnny gives Nick a copy of his single and he plays it on the office stereo. Everyone within earshot seems to dig it. I've heard the song on a cassette in Johnny's room but it booms on a proper hi-fi. The melody reminds me of the classic Who song "The Kids Are Alright," but the sound is much more punk rock, especially when Johnny lays down some power chords in time to the ridiculous catchy chorus that celebrates an amphetamine girl who shines like a pearl.

The three of us decide to go to the famous Marquee Club in Soho where all of the Sixties greats played at one time or another. The headliner tonight is an Irish band called That Petrol Emotion, who include in their ranks Damien and John O'Neill, formerly of The Undertones. They have an American singer named Steve Mack, who according to Nick, dropped out of the University of Washington in Seattle just one month before he was due to graduate and headed to London without any plans. One lucky audition later and he's singing in a band, backed by punk rock legends. Talk about chance luck, or maybe, luck just happens when you take chances.

While waiting for the band to come on we have a few pints and Nick drops a bombshell. "I'm moving to New York," he says. "I just got an amazing job offer from *Spin*."

"Holy shit, that's awesome," says Johnny, beating me to the congratulations. "You have no excuse not to see my band now," he adds while laughing.

"Wow, so you'd take New York over London?" I ask. In my mind, London is the center of the musical universe, and New York is just another big city.

"I love London, but it's an easy choice. I'm scraping by making a living here. *Spin* has a lot more money than *Melody Maker*. It's either that or I'll need to do something else if I stay in London. I don't want to live in a bedsit when I'm thirty like some writers and musicians I know."

I wonder if I'll think the same way when I'm twenty-five. Paul's as old as Nick is and he'll be a professor in a few years. Nick's infinitely cooler than Paul with a school kid's enthusiasm for rock 'n' roll. This is the first time I've heard him talk like a grown up. I buy a round of shots to celebrate Nick's new job. He'll be leaving London in March. I'll miss him but now I'll know two people in New York. It gives me an option when I graduate and can finally get out of Michigan.

That Petrol Emotion is fantastic. Sonically, they're not a million miles apart from The Jesus and Mary Chain. The songs are catchy and substantive with lots of blissful noise, one difference being that like Easterhouse, That Petrol

Emotion has a very pronounced political agenda. This is the second time in a month that I've become exposed to the 'Irish Troubles' via a rock 'n' roll band. I make a mental note to learn more about Ireland and the IRA, but that can wait. Right now I feel at one with my surroundings, enjoying music in a world famous club with two new, but already dear friends.

After the show Nick introduces Johnny and I to the band. Nick seems to know everybody. I manage to ask Steve, who looks like a punk rock surfer with his spiky blonde hair, if he really dropped out of school to come to London and he says, "Yeah, man, it just wasn't for me."

Even though it's not even February, I'm starting to feel under the gun. My mom just mailed me a University of Michigan course catalog for next fall's classes. I don't want to go back to Ann Arbor, but it's not like I've found academic nirvana at Essex either. I'm not Paul. I'll never be a professor, doctor, or lawyer. I fantasize about going AWOL like Steve Mack.

On the train back to Colchester I ask Johnny what he wants to do when he graduates. He says that he figures he'll work at a record store or book store while he gives the band a shot. I ask him what his family thinks, telling him about my parents' great expectations and how they seem disappointed that I don't measure up to my golden boy brother.

"My parents are divorced," says Johnny. "I don't see my dad much. He's a lawyer and probably wants me to do something professional, but my mom's pretty mellow. She teaches English at a high school. You need to do what's right for you anyway. Life's too fucking short to listen to anyone except the voices inside your head."

On the weekend, Julie says that we need to talk, so we take a walk to Wivenhoe to get some quiet time away from the flat. She seems to have read my recent thoughts.

"I don't want to be your English fling," she says. "I'm already thinking about when you'll be going back. I don't want to get hurt again."

"I don't want to go back," I say.

"You've said that before, but you need to do something about it if you're going to stay here."

"If I stay for another year, will you stay in Colchester for another year?"

"Yes," she says. I kiss her and tell her that I love her and that I don't want to lose her. I tell her that I'll try to transfer to Essex and finish school here.

The most difficult part is yet to come. I have to convince my parents.

HANGING ON THE TELEPHONE

On Sunday I phone home at a strategic time when I know my mom and dad will be rested and in a good mood after reading the mammoth Sunday edition of *The New York Times*. My mom answers and per usual she yells to my father to pick up the other phone in their bedroom. They have this annoying habit of talking to me, or, in some cases, talking at me, at the same time.

I start with the good news that I got published in *Melody Maker*; I need to build my case right away.

"What's *Melody Maker*?" my dad asks.

OK, maybe not such a great start. "It's one of the most famous music magazines in the world," I say. "It's like when Paul gets published in a scholarly magazine. Only a lot more people will read what I write." I hope it doesn't sound like a dig, even though it was intended as one.

"Well maybe you should get a graduate degree in journalism," my mom says. In my parents' worldview, advanced degrees are the answer to everything. They're not big on the idea of the self made man or the school of hard knocks. "If only your grades were better you might be able to get into Northwestern. They have a very famous journalism program."

Jesus. I bite my lips before I continue. "You don't need a degree to write about rock 'n' roll. Besides, I don't want to go home in June. I want to transfer from Michigan and finish here. Another year here and I can really make some dents with my writing."

"Michigan is a better school," says my dad. "It will look better on your resume when you apply to graduate schools."

"Look mom and dad, I don't want to go to graduate school. I'm not like you guys and Paul."

"You never try very hard," says my mom. "Paul was always studying and he was always involved with school activities."

"And I won state cross country championships. Paul is an egghead." I know it's not helping my case to bring up Paul, but I'm getting pissed off. "I get it. You don't like it that I don't think the same way as you guys. I can't fake it. The only thing I want to do is become a music journalist. I have a friend in London who just got a job in New York City. If I can't get anything in England, I could probably get a job there. Besides, I met someone."

"Is it serious?" my mom asks.

"Very," I say.

I tell my mom and dad all about Julie; that she's smart, beautiful, and sweet. I tell them that she's going to get a masters degree in English Literature (that wins me some points), and that we're planning on moving in together the next year if I can transfer to Essex.

"And she's OK with you writing about rock 'n' roll?" asks my dad. Despite being the right age in the Sixties, my parents' rock 'n' roll knowledge is pretty much limited to The Beatles. The idea that anyone could make a living writing about a lot of noise is extremely alien to them.

"If I can't make enough money writing, I'll do something else to make ends meet. I've always had summer jobs. I've never been a snob about working."

My parents agree to talk about it, but I don't feel optimistic. My mom keeps asking if I'm sure that I'm not rushing into things with Julie as a way to try to stay in England, and my dad keeps bringing up what he calls the big picture. "It's fine to have fun in college, but the decisions you make now are going to affect your future. You need to think about the big picture."

MAKING PLANS FOR JULIE

Julie accepts a spot in her master's program and I get all the necessary forms from the student admissions office at Essex to initiate the transfer process if my parents give me the OK. They don't. Instead, they give me an ultimatum: that I can finish at Michigan on their dime or find my own way to pay for everything if I stay here. They say that Julie can wait another year.

"If it's serious," says my mom, "the two of you can get together when you graduate. We could even buy you a ticket if you wanted to visit her over Christmas."

I know Julie well enough to know she'll flip out if I tell her this. I lie and say that I can stay another year. I feel shitty, but until I can figure something out, lying seems to be the best option. Julie's already ticked off that I'm going to Europe with Johnny over spring break and more bad news might put her over the edge. The two of us take long walks in Colchester, exploring neighborhoods we might want to live in, always hand in hand. I can sense her excitement as my stomach churns. I feel like I'm going to give myself ulcers if I keep this charade going much longer, but I don't know what else to do.

Julie and I take a train to Chelmsford so she can introduce me to her parents and her younger sister Jill. Julie's been on speaking terms with her mom again now that she's met a nice man. Her parents live in a three-bedroom council flat in a modern suburban development. Though they don't have a lot of money (Julie's education is entirely funded by government grants), the place is immaculate with matching furniture in every room, not an item out of place. Despite the disparities in income, I think it's a safe bet that Julie's family has spent more on their furniture, television, and kitchen appliances than my very well off parents, who have a very bohemian attitude about possessions other than maintaining a vast library.

Julie's parents are polite and proper. Both of them are originally from the north; her father, John, from York, her mother, Sarah, from Leeds. Jill is nineteen and already engaged. Her fiancé, Trevor, is also there. He reminds me of some of the smooth soul boys I see around Colchester, sharp haircuts and neatly pressed clothes, modern updates of the Albert Finney character in the classic film *Saturday Night and Sunday Morning.*

Julie's mom sends the men off to the pub and asks her daughters to help with dinner, so John, Trevor, and I head off to a watering hole nearby called The White Horse. I seem to gain cred with them when I order a John Smith's.

"I thought you Yanks only drank lager," comments Trevor.

"Some Americans like real beer," I say with a smile.

"Plenty of that here at the White Horse," says John. I like the way John says horse with the silent H. "It's my home away from home."

"Come here often then?" I query.

"As much as we can, mate," says Trevor.

"Nothing like the love of a good English lass," says John, "but a man needs a sanctuary."

"And somewhere to hide when they want to take you shopping," complains Trevor. "Jill's already spent more than I can add up."

John laughs. "It only gets worse, son. Only gets worse."

The conversation swings to what I plan to do for a living. Julie's dad is nice enough, but I can tell he looks out for her. He doesn't want her with a layabout. The longer I've been here, the more I realize that the English really like to settle down in a hurry, not leaving the prospects of career, spouse, or home ownership open to chance. Take what you can get as soon as you can get it and hang on for dear life.

Trevor is twenty and he's been out of school for four years. He's an electrician's apprentice and when he receives his full certification, he and Jill plan to get married. In England, the vast majority of students leave school at age sixteen, only a tiny percentage going on to sixth form college for two years to prepare for a further three years of university. I tell them that I have one more year of school and that I plan to be a journalist.

"I'm glad our Julie met you," says John. "She was threatening to leave university for that Matthew lad. It will be a dream come true when she graduates."

"I'm glad she didn't leave early, or else I'd never have met her," I say. "She'll be an excellent teacher, or whatever else she decides to do. She works harder than anyone I know."

"She was always like that," John says. "Always reading, always going to the library for more books. She's never been one to accept her lot in life, always wants something better for herself."

The meal is good and filling, chicken, mashed potatoes, and mushy peas. A good home cooked meal like the ones I had when I was staying with Chris in Newcastle.

Everyone peppers me with questions about America and for about the tenth time on this trip I have to disappoint someone that no, I've never been to Disneyland or Disney World. After a cup of tea, Julie's dad drives us to the train station.

"I'm glad that went well," says Julie after her father leaves. "My dad is always easy going, but it doesn't take much to set my mum off. The last few years with Matthew were like a roller coaster ride."

"I love you," I say squeezing her hand perhaps too tightly. I feel like I really do love Julie, but at this particular moment I really need to hang on to anything. I don't want to go back to America and turn into someone like my parents or Paul.

DON'T YOU WANT ME BABY?

It's an exceptionally warm Sunday in early March and I'm having a cup of tea in the Eddington common area with Julie and Claire, who's popped by to collect Julie on her way to the library. The two of them were going to study that afternoon, while I was planning on watching football on the telly with some flatmates. Dave comes over with a cup of tea and joins us.

He seems to be back to his old self again. For the last month or so he had been making snide ball and chain jokes whenever I mentioned anything about Julie, or even when he saw the two of us together, but now he seems to be at peace with the situation. I'm not sure if it's because he's finally OK with Julie and I being a couple (I can't help but remember what James and Julie told me about him in the past) or if he's simply jealous that Johnny seems to have taken his place as my new best friend. Over the past month, Johnny and I have seen a bunch of shows together: Redskins, The Woodentops, Gene Loves Jezebel, and Sigue Sigue Sputnik all at Essex, and The Dentists and Del Amitri at the Marquee on another London trip. I wrote reviews of all of these shows and though Nick has again relayed to me that *Melody Maker* likes my writing, none of them were published.

As Julie and Claire get up to leave, Dave, out of the blue, asks if we feel like going to Clacton.

"I thought it would be a nice day to go to the seaside," he says.

"I haven't seen the ocean since I've been here," I respond.

"We must go, then," says Claire. "It's too beautiful day of a day to spend in the library. That can wait."

Julie, who's usually pretty Type A about her studies, is equally enthusiastic so it's suddenly a date. Julie and Claire dash over to Claire's room to change into something more beach-worthy, while Dave and I have another cup of tea. We both opt for the jeans and t-shirts we're already wearing, Echo and The Bunnymen for me, The Smiths for Dave. When Julie and Claire come back, Julie is wearing a black skirt and a pink top, while Claire is wearing a floral sleeveless dress and shades. We take a bus from the university to the seaside and spend the afternoon walking along the beach and hanging around on the pier. It's the first day in what feels like forever that I haven't needed to wear my leather jacket. Watching my friends in the sunshine, I realize how damn pale everyone is here, especially Irish Claire.

The amusements are closed for the season, so we mostly see older folks puttering about, none of the typical summer crowd of noisy, sugared up kids and wannabe juvenile toughs. I can't help but think of Morrissey's lyric from "Rusholme Ruffians" about the boy who was stabbed at the last night of the fair by the big wheel generator. Clacton has seen better days. Some of the attractions on the pier have been permanently boarded up and are now wall papered with vulgar sexist and racist graffiti; National Front propaganda mixed in with names of girls who are scrubbers, slags, sluts, and, in one case, a spunk chugger. The Ferris wheel and Merry-Go-Round look old and rusty. I half expect to see signs requiring documented proof of a tetanus shot before boarding.

Faded nostalgia aside, I'm having a blast, almost forgetting that I've been living a lie with Julie for the past few weeks. I need to tell her what my parents said, but I don't know how. Early on we stop for chips and vinegar served the old fashioned British way over newspaper and as the afternoon starts to wind down, we all get 99's, English ice cream cones consisting of vanilla soft serve and a Cadbury Flake chocolate bar inserted in the side.

"99's brings back memories," says Dave. "My parents used to always take me to Blackpool when I was a little kid. I used to love the rides and attractions. Once my dad started making more money we stopped going and always went abroad."

"Such a hard life," teases Claire.

"Where did you go for holidays?" I ask.

"I have family in Killiney, just south of Dublin. We'd go there most summers. It's right on the seaside. It was a nice escape from Belfast."

"I've always wanted to go to Brighton," I say. "I love *Quadrophenia*."

"Me, too," she says. "Brighton's great. You should go if you get a chance."

"I'll try," I say. "I never really liked Sting in *Quadrophenia* though. He doesn't even look like a mod."

"No argument from me," says Dave. "I've always hated The Police and that pretentious wanker, but if you guys want to go to Brighton this summer I'm more than game."

"I always came here," says Julie, bringing everyone back to the present. "Well, at least since my parents moved to Chelmsford."

"I wish I came here," I say, taking her hand. "My parents always took me and my brother to this depressing little resort in the Catskill Mountains."

"I'd like to move to America, someday," says Claire. "California sounds quite appealing. All that sunshine, Disneyland, maybe I'll even meet a cute surfer boy."

Dave laughs. "Had enough with Englishmen, eh?"

"Maybe so," she jests back. "Julie's inspired me," she adds as she gives her friend a pat on the shoulder. "Maybe, I'll meet an American knight in shining armor some time."

We see a pub in the distance and Dave says, "Enough walking for me today. Let's get a pint."

It's still pretty early, barely past seven, but it's close to pitch black now and the winds are starting to gust. England is getting back to being England. I can hear waves crash against the rocks, but can no longer see them. I feel a light ocean mist in the air and as we reach a pub, named after some generic nautical term, the rain comes crashing down. The pub is nice and warm inside. The girls get glasses of wine and Dave and I get cracking on the John Smiths. It's one of those nights where one drink becomes many more and the girls venture over to the jukebox, where time seems to have stopped in 1982. They pick a selection of old hits from the likes of Abba, Bay City Rollers, and David Essex.

When The Human League's "Don't You Want Me" comes on, Claire gets up and starts dancing to the bewilderment of the old couples having quiet Sunday evening drinks. She signals for Julie to join her, but Julie laughs and waves her off. When the song finishes, Claire comes back to the table, pushes back her hair, still wet from the rain and puts on her shades. She impulsively takes my hand and leads me back to the jukebox and selects the song again. She whispers for to me to mimic the Phil Oakey parts while she pretends to be Joanne Catherall, and the two of us drunkenly lip synch to the amused punters and a somewhat horrified Julie and Dave (who seem to be pretty chummy all of a sudden), a tale of how we first met when she was working as a waitress at a cocktail bar. Claire is glowing, looking much cooler than Corey Hart in her sunglasses at night, dancing in the dark in a dive bar in Clacton. She pulls me close for the chorus that Oakey and Catherall sing together, and for an instant I feel like grabbing Claire and kissing her. I'll stop the world and melt with you. The song ends and I'm shocked back to reality.

The four of us miss the last bus home and end up taking a taxi back to campus. Julie is pretty wasted and a little out of her element—usually she's in 'complete control'—and when we get back to the flat we have passionate drunken sex. She wants it fast and now (totally out of character) and I climax harder than I can ever remember.

UNDER A BLOOD RED SKY

It's Friday, two weeks later, and the flat is clearing out as people leave for the month-long spring break. In just a few days, Johnny and I will be heading to the continent. We've marked out an itinerary that will take us through Paris, Venice, and Florence, with a final week in Rome where Johnny will be able to reconnect with Sophia. We'll be traveling with another American named Anthony, who came over for the second semester with Johnny. He's more conservative than the two of us, politically and socially, but seems to be a pretty nice guy.

I'm getting ready to go to London to see Paul. The plan is that we'll meet for dinner and then I'm going to pop by some big going away party for Nick in Camden. I tell Julie that I'm going to crash at Nick's place after the party and I'll see her on Saturday afternoon.

She's pretty pissed off at me today, the first real fight we've had. I try to charm her, but she's not feeling warm and fuzzy right now. I just got a postcard from Christine and absentmindedly left it on my desk where Julie came across it. There was nothing incriminating in it, just another trite snapshot of downtown Ann Arbor, a response to a quick note I sent back in January telling her about the Easterhouse review that got published. The entirety of Christine's message is, "Awesome review. You rock. I always knew great things were in store for you. Love, Christine."

"I thought you were through with her," says Julie.

"I am. She's just a friend."

"Well, why do you still need to be friends?"

"It's better than being enemies," I respond somewhat dryly.

"Sarcasm is the lowest form of wit. This isn't funny to me." I've never seen Julie this pissed off.

"Look, there's nothing going on with me and Christine. She's just a friend now. If you feel better about it I'll just stop talking to her altogether."

As I get up to leave, she asks one last time, "Are you sure there's nothing more you need to tell me? I feel like you're hiding something."

"No," I say, wondering what she might be driving at. "I told you that I'm done with Christine."

Julie lets it go, but I can tell she's still fuming. I try to kiss her, but she turns away and I end up awkwardly pecking her on the cheek. Normally I listen to my Walkman on the train to London, but this time I listen to the sounds of silence as I gaze at Essex suburban life from my window.

Paul is staying at a swank hotel in Hyde Park. I meet him in the lobby at dinnertime. He's just come back from an afternoon seminar and has a full slate of stuff going on tomorrow before heading back to Boston on Sunday. People always say that the two of us look a lot alike and I can finally see that. It's been about two years since we've last seen each other. Paul's tall and thin like I am, but he's much more clean cut. He has short hair with a side part and is quite preppy. Today he's wearing a blue wool blazer with a white dress shirt, a rep tie (probably some club he belonged to at Princeton or Harvard), khakis, and tassel loafers. I've made a bit of an effort for the occasion. I'm wearing a black dress shirt with dark jeans and DM's. Instead of my leather jacket that never seems to leave home without me, I've borrowed Johnny's suit jacket.

The two of us shake hands. Suddenly I feel really glad to see him. It's been too long. Caught up in the emotion, I give Paul a hug. He seems a little surprised at my public display of affection. I am, too, but after my falling out with my parents—I haven't called or written since they told me I couldn't stay here—I feel desperate not to lose him, too.

"It's really great to see you Paul," I say. It feels different seeing him outside of a family setting where everything inevitably turns serious and tense.

"Likewise, Drew. You almost look presentable though I don't know about that hair," he teases.

I've been wearing my hair more like Bobby Gillespie lately, long over the eyes in front, with about one third of my ears covered. The kind of haircut that screamed rebellion when The Rolling Stones first started, but is actually pretty tame in alternative circles these days.

"And you look like you just got back from a regatta, Paul," I tease back.

We walk to a restaurant that one of the professors at the conference recommended to Paul. It's a pretty high-end Italian joint and I'm nervous that they might not let me in wearing jeans, but, unlike the protagonist in one of my favorite Echo and the Bunnymen songs, I'm able to cut the mustard.

"By the way this is all on me, or should I say John Harvard," says Paul as he makes a joke at the expense his university's founder after ordering a pricey bottle of red.

"That's a relief," I say. "I'm not sure if I'm in good enough shape to dine and dash anymore!"

"Not doing any running, eh?"

"Not since I've been here. I was in OK shape over the summer, but it's hard to stay focused when I'm not training for anything. I do walk a lot though. My girlfriend Julie likes to walk."

"She sounds nice. Mom mentioned her to me." My mom always mentions things.

"I hope everything works out," he adds.

"Me too," I say. I don't tell him about my recent fight with our mom and dad. I ask how his fiancé Caroline is doing. Paul and Caroline met at Princeton and they both went to Harvard together. She just finished law school and now works for some big firm in Boston.

"She's doing really well," Paul says. "I feel like we

never see each other though. She works like eighty hours a week, no exaggeration, and this dissertation has taken over my life. On top of that, I'm also teaching a couple of classes this spring."

"Suddenly I feel really lazy," I reply.

Changing the subject, I bite the bullet and ask, "Do you know why mom and dad seem so opposed to me staying in England? I get the feeling that they don't trust my judgment. I really love Julie and I really want to stay here. Going back to Michigan would be a nail in the coffin. I can't see the relationship working long distance."

"I actually took your side on that. I think I almost gave them a heart attack. If you're doing so well with your writing, you probably have a future in it. If England is the best place to pursue it you should. It's not like mom and dad don't have the money. They're just scared."

"I just can't be something that I'm not. Do I really seem like the grad school type?"

"Not really," says Paul with a laugh. "Despite their liberal intentions, mom and dad can be pretty one dimensional. You don't want to know how much pressure I felt in junior high and high school. I felt like they were academic equivalents of little league coaches."

"Damn, I never knew they were like that with you. They kind of left me alone when they realized I wasn't going to be a 4.0 student. I mean they'd make digs but they didn't force me to do homework or anything. Second child syndrome or something; they probably stopped caring so much. They seem to be getting a second wind now that I'm almost finished with college."

Our dinner arrives and Paul orders another bottle of wine. It's kind of surreal to get buzzed with Paul, but it feels good to let go of some of the old demons, which seem kind of silly now. I can live with Paul being an academic superstar and Paul seems cool with me. I just want my mom and dad to be on my side.

Paul asks if I ever miss running. "That seemed to be

your whole identity. I was almost expecting to see you lining up at the front of the Boston Marathon after you finished college. What made you just stop?"

"It's really hard to explain. I still have dreams where I'm racing and I wake up thinking I'm still a runner and then I remember I'm not. It happened so fast. I wanted to take a break when things weren't going well my freshman year and the coach more or less gave me an ultimatum to quit or else. Before I knew it, I was hanging out with a different crowd and partying all the time."

"Mom and dad were always worried about that. They thought your friend PJ was a bad influence."

"And they didn't know half of it." I tell him some tales. I'm pretty loopy from the wine and it feels easy to open up.

Paul seems pretty amazed. "In some ways I'm kind of jealous," he says. That surprises me.

He continues, "I've always tried to do everything by the book. I've never really let go. Other than being wine connoisseurs, Caroline and I have always been pretty ordinary. I really love what I'm doing—I know you might find that hard to believe—but I'm well aware that I'm becoming the cliché of the limousine liberal type. In five or ten years we'll probably have two kids in private schools I can barely afford and living in some exclusive Boston suburb."

"I'm scared that I'm going to be thirty, living in a studio apartment, and barely scraping a living as a rock journalist."

"You don't see yourself getting married or anything?"

"It's too weird to think that far ahead. Julie practically lives in my dorm room now and as far as she knows, we're looking for an apartment to move into. I don't know what to do…"

"You need to tell her the truth. If she loves you, you'll work it out. I'll try to work on mom and dad some more, but you owe Julie the truth, even if it sucks."

"You're right, Paul. I'll tell her tomorrow."

I walk with Paul back to his hotel. He gives me some cash for a cab. "You don't want to be riding around on the subway at night," he says.

"It's not too bad," I say, but I'm not going to argue. We say goodbye and he promises to call mom and dad and plead my case some more.

I try to remember the last time I had this much fun with Paul and my mind takes me back to a summer in the Catskills. I was about to begin fifth grade and Paul was about to start high school. When my friends weren't around, our mom and dad would often make Paul look after me, especially in the summer when they were both working during the day. I'd tag along with him and his friends and he'd try not to be too annoyed, but this time he seemed glad to have me around.

The place we stayed at in the Catskills was a resort that had seen better times, a haven for Ukrainian-Americans, who tried to desperately hang on to memories of the old country. Unlike the other kids staying there, Paul and I didn't speak Ukrainian (my parents only paid lip service to the old country crap), so we got pretty tight, especially one day when a girl Paul was trying to impress started babbling and giggling with some of her friends in the mother tongue. We were in the resort's basement recreation room, which was decorated with the full on wood paneling that was so fashionable at the time. They had a few pool tables, an air hockey table, and a jukebox with some current hits and a lot of old standards. The girl who Paul was trying to score with was a cute blonde who wore too much cheap perfume and had feathered hair like Farrah Fawcett on *Charlie's Angels*. She kept playing this sappy song about a horse named "Wildfire." I hated that song with a passion and kept counteracting with Queen's "Killer Queen" when her selection would finish. This went on at least four or five times in a row before the girl finally ran out of quarters and left the room in a huff. When she was gone, the two of us started laughing hysterically. It was our small, silly victory over the Ukrainian kids.

I cab it to Camden and find Nick's going away party.

It's at a pub called The Falcon and a band from Australia called The Moodists are on stage. When Nick sent the invite, he wrote that I'd probably like them because they're "all dark and gloomy" and they do sound pretty good in a Nick Cave kind of way I think as I order a pint at the bar and walk over to the table where Nick and his crowd have gathered. I already feel a little like the odd man out since Nick is the only one in the group I actually know and they're all reliving stories about the good old days. At one point, I manage to get a few words in with Nick and ask why none of my reviews are getting published.

Suddenly, he seems pretty uncomfortable. "Do you know someone named David Browne?" he asks.

"Yeah," I say. "He's my friend. He lives in my flat."

"Are you sure he's a mate?"

This is getting weird. "Of course," I say. Thick as thieves, Dave once said.

"Look, I hate to say this to you, then. Dave's the reason you're not getting anything published. His mate Liam is an editorial assistant to my boss Travis and from what I was told, you apparently have been talking a lot of smack about *Melody Maker* and how it's a crap paper. I don't believe it, but Travis seems to."

"Christ, I can't believe that! Nick, you know it's not true." I'm practically crying.

"I know it's not. Look Travis is here if you want to try to sort things out."

"I'm not in the mood now." I feel like throwing myself in front of some train tracks.

"I will then," says Nick. "Look, I'm really sorry. Come to New York next year. I'll try to sort you out with *Spin*, fresh start for both of us."

It's all starting to make sense. It's not that Dave accepted my relationship with Julie; he just found a way to fuck me while secretly sitting back in contentment, watching my hard work go down the toilet. My Easterhouse review and the fact that I invited Johnny to come celebrate with Nick in

London and not him—it must have set things off. I'm fuming and trying to think of the last time I was in a fight.

New York is starting to sound like a good escape. The English noose around my neck is starting to get too tight. I need to confront Dave and, more pressingly, I need to tell Julie that barring a miracle I'm going back to America in June. I decide to go to Liverpool Street and catch the midnight train to Colchester. He's leaving on that midnight train to Colchester, I sing to myself. Doesn't have the same dynamic ring as the Gladys Knight hit, but the sentiment is the same. I don't belong in London. Suddenly, I hate this fucking place. I look around at Nick's table one last time and feel like glassing all the candy ass limeys. I decide to save the rage for Dave.

It's 3:00am when I get back to Eddington. I hear music coming from Dave's room but otherwise it's dead quiet. I want to confront him, but decide to talk to Julie first. Julie's not in my room, but it's a huge mess. All the papers on my desk have been thrown on the floor and I can see a lot of ripped up pages from my notebook. Fuck. The glossy of Christine is ripped in half. Fuck. All the postcards she sent that I neatly tucked in one of the notebook's folders are also ripped apart. Fuck. I sit on the floor and try to decipher what she's read. Pretty much everything, I decide. While most of the notebook was just a diary of concerts I went to and records I bought, I also wrote some pretty personal stuff in there. I piece together some sheets from an entry that I wrote after I had sex with Julie the first time. I emoted that while it was more intimate being with Julie I missed the spontaneity I had with Christine. Fuck. There's also a torn page from where I rant about my parents not wanting me to stay at Essex. How long has Julie known that I've been lying to her?

I wonder if Dave knows where she is. He does. When I open the door, Julie is in his bed. I want to beat him to a pulp, but I'm too paralyzed to do anything but leave in disgust. The fucking deer in the headlights cliché has come to life and I feel like I've been steamrolled by a semi. I slam the door. I can hear Julie yelling something at me, but I don't stop.

I walk aimlessly though the empty university campus. I wonder if Johnny is up. Maybe I should stop by his room? I decide to wait till morning. I gravitate towards Wivenhoe, feeling like Caine in *Kung Fu*, a TV series I enjoyed as a kid, a man walking with no possessions in search of the simple truth. I wonder if Caine ever got screwed over by a British bitch. After a few minutes on the hilly terrain, I decide that Wivenhoe Park is as far as I feel like going. I sit down with my back against a tree and stare off into space. The Essex sky always seems to have this weird red and orange tinge, especially in the twilight hours. I keep staring at the stars and watch the night slowly morph into day. As the sun begins to rise, the sky looks almost blood red.

I awaken to the sound of footsteps and crunching leaves. I open my eyes. It's morning. I must have dozed off. I straighten to an upright position, using the tree trunk for support, and wipe the drool off my face. A group of laughing schoolboys running cross country zip by me, one of them yelling, "Oi, watch it drunkie." I feel like shouting back at him, something on the lines of "I can still run faster than you, wanker," but I just laugh instead. Once a runner…

I get up and go to Johnny's flat. His advice is simple. "Just drop that bitch. Don't listen to any excuses. She's going to make it all about you and how it's your fault."

I'm shaking, especially my hands, and I'm holding back tears, a real fucking mess. Johnny hands me a bottle of Jack Daniels to ice my nerves and I take a few slugs; Breakfast of Champions.

"And don't beat up Dave too badly. You don't want to get kicked out of the country," he adds with a snicker. I finally smile a little.

"I'm happy to leave on my own free will, like tomorrow."

"Not until we go to Italy, man. The women are beautiful there. Julie will seem like a bad dream after that trip."

Johnny gives me an extra pillow and I sleep on his floor until noon. He's gone when I wake up but leaves a note saying, "Gotta go to the library. Let's hit the Hex at 7:00 and the Union Bar after that."

I head back to Eddington. Dave should be gone by now. I really don't want to confront him in this state—between Julie and *Melody Maker*, I'm scared I might actually kill him before I remember he beat the crap out of a random stranger at The Hacienda. Hopefully Julie will have gathered up her stuff from my room by now and be gone, too.

No such luck. She's there.

"Why the fuck are you still here?" I yell. I notice that she's picked up everything and even made the bed, as if nothing had happened.

"Because we need to talk."

"About fucking what?" I can't remember if I've ever yelled like this before, especially at a girl.

"About honesty," she retorts. "You lied to me about Christine, about staying at Essex, pretty much everything."

"So a revenge fuck makes us even?"

"I didn't fuck him. I was upset. I read your notebook and found all the cards from that dirty slag Christine. I asked you if there was anything more you needed to tell me yesterday and you said no. You lied to me."

Christ. She must have gone through my stuff days ago, maybe weeks ago, and held it all in, waiting for an opportune time to strike.

She continues, "When you left, I went to the pub and I ran into Dave and we got really drunk. We just kissed and cuddled a bit." Her tone when she says "kissed and cuddled a bit" is calm and matter of fact, as if she were describing some mundane task like washing the dishes. I don't really hear any remorse. She sounds cold and distant, border line sociopathic. I don't know if I believe her about the just kissing and cuddling part, this is way too much to take in. If it was anyone else, maybe I could forgive her, but Dave?

"I don't feel like talking anymore," I say.

"So you'd rather end up with some tart like Christine?"

"Christine might be a lot of things but at least she's

not a spiteful bitch like you are."

She slaps me. "We could have worked this out." She's crying. "You could have told me the truth about not being able to stay in Essex. I would have followed you to America. I still would."

She's bawling but I don't console her. My pride's too hurt to be chivalrous.

She continues to make her case, "That's all you have to say? We can make it work again. I know we can."

"I don't trust you."

"You're talking to me about trust?!" She's yelling and crying at the same time. "You kept so much secret from me. I've never lied to you."

"You read my fucking diary. A man's entitled to his private thoughts."

"Not when they're hurtful."

She packs up her clothes and books in a flustered panic and finally leaves.

WHAT SHE SAID

    I go the Union Bar for a pint and a shepherd's pie. One pint turns into five and I realize it's almost time to meet Johnny for dinner. I've been stewing over some of the things Julie said to me; does being in a relationship really mean being 100% honest all the time? Do I really have to expose so much of myself to someone to make it work? I assumed that by not telling Julie everything, I was doing her a favor, shielding her from things until I could work it all out. I wonder what Christine is doing.

    It always seems to come back to Christine. I can never leave her behind and I have this destructive habit of conveniently forgetting the hurt she put me through in the past. I'll be your plastic toy. I'm not sure if it's because she was my first love and I just can't or won't let her go, or if the distance apart has badly clouded my memory like one of those lethal Fog Cutter cocktails at a Chinese restaurant. I thought I kicked my Christine habit, but the feelings are still lingering. Spending time with Julie kept the demons at bay, but even then, Christine had this way of skulking her way back into my heart, this time instilling some psychic voodoo revenge on Julie. Well, not Christine literally, but my damn feelings about Christine that poured from pen onto paper, feelings that should have stayed in my heart.

    I decide to call Christine. I realize that maybe I never wanted to let her go in the first place, but is she stringing me along from her puppet master outpost in Ann Arbor, or does she mean it this time? You don't send a guy a glossy S&M photo in the mail if he's in the friend zone, or do you? I need to sack up and find out for sure. Do it clean. I do a drunken time zone calculation. Good chance she might be around. She is.

I thank her for the card and photo and tell her that I really need to talk to her.

"OK," she says, probably wondering what the hell is going on in my head.

I tell her everything. No more mistakes like I made with Julie. I lay it all on the line. I tell her about the weird one-night stand at the warehouse party, watching Dave beat up a guy at The Hacienda, the other one-night stands I had in Ann Arbor when I was trying to forget about her, and everything about Julie. I tell Christine how I tried to make plans to stay in England for another year to be with a girl, a girl who slept with my best friend. I know that I must be sounding like a little melodramatic bitch, but it feels good to get it all out, the emotional equivalent of sticking a finger down my throat when I've had too much to drink. I try to hypothesize to her that maybe I had to go through all of this to realize that she was the right girl all along.

"I know this is way too much to be saying on the phone, but I love you, Christine. I guess I never stopped loving you."

She's crying.

"I'm sorry," I say. "I've said way too much."

"It's not that," she says. "I've met someone."

I don't respond, so she continues. "It happened so fast. We just met and I'm totally in love. We're moving to Los Angeles in June. And he's not a musician," she adds, as if that will somehow console me.

I'm crying, she's crying. It's like a bad after school special about doomed young lovers.

"We weren't really right for each other Drew. I let myself fantasize a bit when I saw you again and we exchanged letters, but what I have for him is real. It really is. I have a chance for a new life in California. It's too good to pass up. God, don't hate me. I'm so sorry."

"I'll live," I lie. Right now I feel like drinking myself into oblivion.

"I'll always be your friend," she says.

I know she won't be. I know this is the last time we'll ever speak.

TOO CASH

The night before we embark on our European adventure, Johnny decides that I really need to see Hüsker Dü at the Electric Ballroom in London. He says it will be good for my soul. I've been digging *Flip Your Wig*, and, as Johnny says, "Nothing like a loud rock 'n' roll show to get a girl out of your system." In my case, I need to exorcise two. Maybe I loved England, or some romantic idea of England, more than Julie herself. She seemed like the right girl on paper, but, deep down, she wasn't the right girl in my heart. I wouldn't have held on to such strong feelings for Christine if she were true. My love for Christine felt genuine, but like all unrequited love it nearly buried me alive and now I have to claw my way back to the surface.

Johnny books a hotel in Camden near the venue and we tell Anthony to meet us at Victoria Station the next day, where the three of us will catch a train to Dover before taking a ferry to Calais, France. Anthony has no interest in seeing Hüsker Dü. He's a massive Police fan; that's as edgy as he gets.

I've been obsessing over certain songs lately to deal with the new-found pain; usual suspects like Prefab Sprout "When Love Breaks Down," Lloyd Cole and The Commotions "Are You Ready To Be Heartbroken?" and The Smiths "Pretty Girls Make Graves." Nick Cave has just released a covers album called *Kicking Against The Pricks* and on the top of my heartbreak hotel playlist is his take on "By The Time I Get To Phoenix," which I play on loop. "By The Time I Get To Phoenix" has been one of my favorite songs forever. When I was in fifth grade, Glen Campbell had this huge hit with "Rhinestone

Cowboy." Instead of just buying the 45, fate somehow intervened and I opted for a greatest hits album that included that song and about a dozen more. I would later learn, as I got more clued in to rock 'n' roll history, that the best songs on that collection —"Galveston," "Wichita Lineman," and "By The Time I Get To Phoenix"—were all written by a young gent from Oklahoma named Jimmy Webb. Cave's version is the best I've heard. It's a poignant narrative of a man who's finally had enough and leaves his ungrateful, cheating woman behind. The protagonist of the song is driving, presumably away from Los Angeles, and, at different stages of the song, imagines what she's up to. When he's in Phoenix, she'll be rising; in Albuquerque she'll be working and wondering where he is when he doesn't answer the phone; and by the time he reaches Oklahoma, she'll be crying herself to sleep because she didn't think he'd really go. Male empowerment neatly condensed into a three-minute pop ballad, at least that's what I keep trying to tell myself.

Johnny and I hang out in Soho and Camden that afternoon, soaking in the scenery, watching the punks strut like John Travolta in *Saturday Night Fever*. They remind me of cartoon characters, sporting colored Mohawks and t-shirts championing third-tier bands like The Exploited and The Adicts. I've always found it funny that no one in the original and best punk bands like The Sex Pistols, Clash, and Damned wore Mohawks, but now it's become an obligatory part of the costume.

After a pub meal in Camden, Johnny and I walk over to the Electric Ballroom. It's a somewhat majestic venue with a capacity of about a thousand. Outside of seeing The Cult at the Ipswich Odeon back in October, all of the gigs I've seen in England have been at dive bars and small clubs. The Electric Ballroom is perfect for Hüsker Dü's vast sound. I'm amazed at how much power the trio generates. The songs roar like jet planes on takeoff as the guitarist and co-vocalist, Bob Mould, jumps around the stage like a big happy teddy bear, albeit one strapped to a Flying V guitar. Grant Hart beats the shit out of the drums so hard that I can practically see the sweat flying off his face, even more so on the songs that he sings from behind his kit. The bass player, Greg Norton, manages to coolly and calmly keep things in control, looking very much like a Seventies gay porn star with his borderline molester mustache. I would later learn, ironically, that he was actually the only straight one in the bunch!

Since *Flip Your Wig* is the only Hüsker Dü album I own, I only recognize about half of the songs in the set, but it's all a fantastic rush. The English kids are eating it up, jumping up and down and moshing like it's the greatest show on earth. The best part of the gig is near the end when the band kicks into a phenomenal version of The Byrds' hippie classic "Eight Miles High." When I was a kid I thought the song was about getting stoned, but on a long trail run with Richie, he explained that it was actually about The Byrds' first trip to England, when everything went wrong. The British press and public weren't digging the band back then. The eight miles high bit literally referred to the band's reflections of the trip as they flew back to friendlier confines in southern California. The Hüsker Dü version is twice as fast and heavy and it knocks the crowd senseless. I conjure up an image of Rocky Balboa pounding carcasses in the meat locker. This is Hüsker Dü saying fuck you to England on my behalf.

Johnny and I are pumped sky high from the show and need to let off a little steam. The pubs are still open and that seems like our best bet until we see a small crowd lining up outside a snooty little nightclub. We can hear Prince's "When Doves Cry" blaring from inside. The punters are slick, the guys opting for New Romantic fashions like baggy suits and silk shirts, while the girls are in short tight skirts, 'fuck me' heels, and skimpy tops. We're both in jeans, t-shirts, and leather jackets, but decide to press our luck. After five or ten minutes we get to the front of the queue. The door man isn't impressed. He's wearing a turquoise suit that Don Johnson might kill for and a black silk shirt, at least three buttons undone. His hair is slicked back and he's wearing Ray-Bans even though it's half past ten.

"A bit too cash, lads, a bit too cash," says the doorman as he blocks our way.

"Pardon?" replies Johnny.

"You're too cash. I'm not letting you in."

"What do you mean, too cash?" I ask. We're pretty confused. "We have money if that's what you're worried about."

"Oi, mate I said cash, as in casual. You're a bit too cash. No jeans! Move along lads, move along."

With the nightclub out of the question, we find a pub near the hotel. At the bar we notice a guy who's probably in his mid-thirties with an American accent talking to a very young British blonde. He has shoulder length blonde hair that looks damaged from spending too much time in the sun and chlorinated swimming pools. He looks and speaks a lot like Sean Penn's character, Jeff Spicoli, from *Fast Times At Ridgemont High*, a total surfer dude.

"*The Big Chill* is probably the worst movie ever made," we hear Spicoli rant to anyone within earshot. His chick seems disinterested as she gazes down on her Babysham. "Fuckin' baby boomers piss me off."

"Amen to that brother," says Johnny.

"I thought it sucked too," I say, "but, hey, the characters all went to the University of Michigan, so I have to give props for that."

"You from Ann Arbor?" asks Spicoli.

"Yeah."

"I've passed through there a few times," Spicoli says. "It's one of the last bastions for freaks. Hope it doesn't change too much. I love that Schoolkids' Records."

"Me too, man, even though a girl who worked there broke my heart." I seem to have to tell everyone my life story now.

"No need to fret, brother," says Spicoli. "Chicks come and go. You got to ride the waves of life like the Silver Surfer. You're going to have good days and bad days, but man, you gotta keep on living. Embrace pain and embrace joy. You're either alive or dead, man; anything in between and you're just existing."

Spicoli is pretty wasted but his hippie babble is endearing.

"Guess you're right," I say. "Ann Arbor is still pretty cool, but there seem to be a lot more yuppies and preppies now than when I was a little kid."

"They're everywhere, dude. You guys need to be careful. Your generation needs to do something or people will still be listening to the fucking Beatles and Motown in the year 2000." He pauses, as if he's said something as extreme as the Russians have just landed (in his world view that would probably be the lesser of two evils), and takes a drag from a Marlboro before sipping on some more beer.

"What brings you chaps to London?" Spicoli asks in a faux English accent.

"We're here for study abroad programs," says Johnny. "We're at Essex in Colchester." Johnny sips from his pint and continues, "We just got back from an amazing show at the Electric Ballroom, Hüsker Dü."

"Good band, man," says Spicoli. "I've seen those cats before."

I don't know whether to believe this guy or not. He seems to have been everywhere and done everything, but I agree with him about the damn yuppies and their hippie music. I've always loved that Clash lyric about no Beatles, Rolling Stones, or Elvis in 1977, but punk's moment seems to have faded and the bands I love now only have niche followings. Iggy Pop and David Bowie are still cool because they've rolled with the changes, but I hate the last few Rolling Stones albums (*Undercover* was an abomination) and they used to be my favorite band. God knows how bad they might sound if they decide to make any more records.

"So what do you do?" Johnny asks Spicoli.

"As little as possible, man. My philosophy is to die. You know, do-it-easy," he says, slowly enunciating the three words that make up the acronym.

Johnny and I laugh.

"I like it, man," says Johnny.

"What about you cats?" asks Spicoli. "You don't look like you want to be yuppies."

"I'm in a band," says Johnny. "Music is my thing."

"Right on," says Spicoli.

"I'm a writer," I say.

"Well, it's up to you to tell the truth then, brother."

Spicoli signals to his girl that he's ready to leave and she grabs her coat. Johnny and I are in hysterics. This dude has some kind of Manson magic with the ladies.

"Gotta groove dudes," says Spicoli. "Nice to meetcha. Don't let death get in the way of your dreams."

Spicoli and the leggy blonde make their exit. Johnny and I order another round. "Now that guy was way too cash," Johnny says.

MUSHY PEAS IN PARIS

Johnny and I are still buzzing from the gig and the wacky conversation we had with Spicoli when we meet Anthony at Victoria Station. Anthony's a short, skinny Italian-American guy, who goes to Columbia. He's super friendly but way too serious. Johnny met him on their flight over to London in January and said that all Anthony talked about was the law schools he planned to apply to. At the platform Anthony even tells us that he may leave Rome early to get in some more studying. Anthony's pretty useful though. He's printed out itineraries for us to follow as we navigate our way through Paris, Venice, Florence, and Rome.

"What if we want to wing it a bit?" asks Johnny, pointing to a sign he sees for a hovercraft trip available from Dover to the Netherlands.

"Oh no," says Anthony, "I've planned everything. I know you guys won't want to go to all the museums and sites that I want to go to, but I'll freak out if I don't stick to a plan."

We let it slide, though I have a feeling that we'll be teasing Anthony some more on this trip. He's too much of the perfect poster boy for America's Reagan youth not to. The train ride to Dover is scenic and it reminds me of the ending of *Quadrophenia*, when the protagonist Jimmy starts to flip out on the train to Brighton as he runs away from London after his girlfriend leaves him for his best friend (who was coincidently also named Dave). Jimmy steals a scooter from a character played by Sting and drives it off a huge cliff. I don't feel that out of control, but another few weeks in Old England and I just might.

The cassette I have on my Walkman is keeping me at bay for the moment. It's a demo tape by a band called Spacemen 3 that Nick passed on to me. I don't know anything about these guys. Later, in another life I'll know everything about them and interview one of the co-songwriters, Sonic Boom, on a beautiful sunny afternoon in Los Angeles. The two of us will share multiple cups of tea and chat as Sonic rolls countless handmade cigarettes with his skeleton thin fingers. The name of the tape is intriguing, *For All The Fucked Up Children In The World, We Bring You Spacemen 3*, and the band has a little bit of everything I love in them; the noisy power and grace of The Stooges, some Jesus and Mary Chain distortion in all the right places, and an overall Anglo blues vibe that reminds me of the Rolling Stones when Brian Jones steered the ship. Two particular favorites are "Walking With Jesus" and a lengthy opus called "Fixin' To Die," where the singer pleads to his Lord to help him because he's been on smack. Despite the Jesus fixations, Spacemen 3 doesn't seem to be religious in the way U2 used to be like on "Rejoice" or "Fire." These guys aren't testifying. This is straight up gospel and blues-infused rock 'n' roll. Spacemen 3 is coming from a similar place to Nick Cave, deathbed confessionals and all that jazz.

On the ferry to Calais, we're too tired to catch any shuteye, so the three of us hang out with a group of French girls and drink wine. I sink a Valium. I'm finally running out of my stash, so I take it pretty sparingly these days. Might be time to see a shrink again and get a refill; milk the breakup with Julie for some chemical stimulation. The girls know a little English, but we know no French, so the conversation is minimal. The vibe is nice though, young people having fun like we're supposed to.

We take another train from Calais to Paris and get there super early, like 7:00am. The hotels and B&B's won't be open to take reservations for at least another hour, so we go to a park. Anthony tries to get some sleep on a bench, while Johnny and I try to annoy him with faux French accents based on the cartoon character Pepe Le Pew.

Later, we book four nights at a scuzzy joint called the Hotel Clauzel that's centrally located near Notre Dame Cathedral—the only real selling point. The place is run by a couple of shady looking Middle Eastern guys who are having coffee with some other shady looking Middle Eastern guys who are smoking cigarettes. Where's Rambo or Chuck Norris when you need them? One of the guys tosses me a key that has a barely visible number etched into it. "Floor Four, you go there," he says in pigeon English. The elevator isn't working so we hoof it up the stairs and enter an open room that looks clean enough minus the peeling wallpaper. The three of us immediately collapse into comatose states.

A loud noise awakens me. I don't know how long I've been asleep. It could have been three minutes or three hours. I see some figures standing above me, yelling in a tongue I can't decipher. Am I still dreaming? I try to focus. I recognize a couple of the guys from downstairs. Are they going to rob us, or worse, maybe even kill us? Fuck. They start yelling. Johnny and Anthony are awake too. Anthony looks like he's possibly pissed himself. One of the Arabs seems to be packing something. Could it be a knife or even a gun? I'm groggy from the lack of sleep and hung over from last night's cocktail of Valium and low quality ferry wine. I feel sluggish and defenseless.

One of the Arabs finally explains in broken English that we're sleeping in the wrong room. We misread the number on the key! The three of us laugh, get up and haul our stuff to the right room. We're too jacked up to sleep any more so we go out in search of food. We see some Americans walking into a nearby McDonald's and Johnny and I start to laugh.

Johnny says, "No wonder everyone in the world hates us."

Anthony isn't too thrilled. He's actually a Republican, which is a little fascinating. On the ferry he was telling us how Reagan was the greatest American president ever and that more Americans needed to be full of ingenuity and integrity like Lee Iacocca. Johnny and I just cringed.

We find a cozy little bistro, but soon our lunch experience becomes almost as weird as the hotel check in. The food is OK, but, for some reason, all of our dishes include a side order of mushy peas that are just plain awful. You'd think we were in Yorkshire or something. When the waiter sees that we won't be cleaning off our plates, he gets livid. We try to feed him some crap about being too full to eat anything else, but he isn't buying it.

Fortunately the rest of our stay in Paris is relaxing. We do a lot of the touristy things and I enjoy it; Eiffel Tower, Notre Dame, a long walk through the South Bank and several museums, including The Louvre. I always hated going to museums as a kid, but I feel like I could spend hours in The Louvre, at least looking at one painting in particular that has a strange and powerful hold over me. It's an early nineteenth century piece by a Frenchman named Girodet called *The Entombment of Atala*. My eyes lock on the image of a young long-haired man clinging desperately to his dead lover's knees as a priest tries to drag her away. I've never lost anyone to death, but the imagery strikes a chord, more than any work of art or even any song has. I think about Julie and Christine and just the concept of loss in general. Life is full of moments that you want to hold on to forever (I wonder if that's what the Psychedelic Furs were thinking about when they called their album *Forever Now*). I tell Johnny and Anthony to meet me in a half an hour. I need to spend some more time with Mr. Girodet.

STARING AT THE FRAT BOYS

Venice looks and feels like another planet, one that I could easily slink off to and never leave. The city attracts a lot of tourists, but it doesn't feel like a tourist trap. It's too strange and unique for that. Venice has this fascinating network of narrow canals and winding cobblestone streets that more often than not seem to dead end on us with no warning, as if they were part of some elaborate maze forged during the Renaissance, hopefully sans Minotaur, to trick future visitors. Even Anthony, he of the rigid itineraries, is pretty relaxed and just rolls with it, not minding when we have to backtrack and recalculate our steps. We manage to hit some obvious 'must-see' spots like the St. Mark's Plaza and Anthony takes a gondola ride—Johnny and I refuse—but mainly the three of us just relax, which means coffee, pizza, pasta, and wine, lots of red, red wine.

On our second day in Venice, as the gorgeous Italian sun starts to set, I notice a backwards fraternity baseball cap bobbing in a crowd, totally ruining the sublime moment. I mumble something to Johnny about how it seems like you can't go anywhere in the world without running into douche bag fraternity brothers.

"Yeah, dudes like that belong in Cancun or Fort Lauderdale," says Johnny. "Not anywhere with culture."

He's looking sharp today, like Paul Weller on holiday, in aviator sunglasses, a red Fred Perry shirt with white trim, nicely tailored black trousers and a pair of immaculately polished Brogues. I'm dressed more casually (too cash?) in shades, Psychedelic Furs t-shirt, and Chuck Taylors, while

Anthony is proudly representing the moral majority in a green Ralph Lauren polo, khaki shorts, and boat shoes, no socks, of course.

"Hey, I think I know those guys you're talking about," says Anthony. "They're from Essex. They came over from De-Pauw in January. They're actually pretty cool."

Anthony seems pretty excited and runs up to one of the guys, Jeff, who's with two of his frat buddies, Chip and Jim. I know the faces, but I've never talked to any of them on campus.

"Nice t-shirt, man," says Jeff. "The Psychedelic Furs are my favorite band."

"No shit," I say, taken aback. He doesn't seem the type. Jeff's your standard athletic blonde, blue-eyed all-American frat boy with a conservative haircut, side part and all. Chip is also clean cut but on the scrawnier side; his baseball cap seems too big for his head and he comically keeps fidgeting with it to prevent it from falling forward too much. Jim is a huge guy with a buzz cut who kind of looks like Wally from *Leave It To Beaver*. He probably grew up on a farm in Nebraska or Iowa. Wearing a DePauw Football t-shirt, khaki shorts, and a backwards fraternity cap, he keeps spitting Skoal into a plastic cup.

They're all looking for a place to get some beers and we decide to join them. Normally Johnny and I would never hang with guys like that, but with our lack of any language skills other than Johnny's above average Spanish—which allows us to wing it pretty well in most situations—it's nice to have some real conversation.

Johnny and I shared a nice bottle of red on our last afternoon in Paris, while Anthony went back to see Notre Dame Cathedral for a second time. Over the last few days I've tried not to talk to him about my problems (the general atmosphere in Venice seems to have helped a ton) and make it more about him as the Rome leg of our tour approaches. I can tell that he has it pretty good for Sophia. He says they slept together in Spain last summer, but all the distance apart has made things weird, which is exactly why I didn't want to do the long distance thing with Julie. Johnny and Sophia exchange letters every few weeks and talk on the phone, but he says that it's not really a relationship.

"One of us has to make the move, otherwise it's all bullshit. I've never known of any long distance relationship that's worked," he said.

"Me neither."

"I'll know how I feel when I see her again. I seem to have his spider sense about chicks and if they're into me or not. She used to tell me that she wanted to come to New York to study, but she doesn't mention that any more, which makes me think maybe there's someone else."

"We're too young to be worrying about this shit," I responded. "I had a lot of fun in the fall when I just lived for the moment."

"A toast to women, the best and worst thing about life," said Johnny as the two of us clinked our glasses.

Our Venice entourage finds a sidewalk café that sells Peroni by the bottle; the perfect tonic for a warm spring evening. We go through several rounds, each taking turns to go inside and use the ridiculously small urinal in back to relieve ourselves. I wish I could understand the graffiti on the wall. I haven't eaten much today, other than a slice of pizza, and I'm pretty buzzed.

Jeff says that he wanted to talk to me because I'm always wearing cool band t-shirts, but that whenever he saw me I was always with that pretty British chick.

"Not anymore," I say.

"Sorry to hear that."

"It's OK. I was even going to try to transfer to Essex to be with her."

"Damn, you must have really liked her to commit to that," says Chip.

"I really did, or at least I thought I did. It's weird how isolated I've become here. It makes me question most of my decisions lately. I've been here since October but it feels like

I've been here forever."

"Yeah one semester is enough for me," says Jeff. "I'm glad I didn't come for the whole year."

"Me too," says Chip.

"I wish I could have been here for a year," says Johnny, the only one who agrees with me. "Life's too short to get bogged down in routines. I wish I had more time to find myself."

"My dad says if I ever try to find myself, he'll kick my ass," says football player Jim, who's been pretty quiet until now. Everyone laughs. It sounds really funny coming out of left field like that.

"I think I'm just going to take a year off school next year," I say. "I don't want to be at Essex for another year, but I can't see myself back at Michigan in the fall either."

"You should come to New York, then," says Johnny. "You can manage my band!"

"$50 says you'll both be doing pretty normal things in a few years," counteracts Jeff. "It happens to the best of us."

He continues, "You probably just think I'm just some douche bag frat guy, but I like a lot of the same music that you guys do. You can still embrace culture without rebelling against everything."

"You're getting too fucking heavy for me," says Jim. "I feel like swimming across the canal."

"Now I would give $50 to see you do that!" says Jeff.

"Me too," I say.

"I'm in," says Johnny.

The six of us pull together a pile of loose change that probably adds up to a bit more than $50 in U.S. currency and we put Jim to the test.

"Are you really going to do this, dude?" asks Chip.

"Yeah, man," says Jim as he belches loudly. It's dark now and not too many people are wandering around. Jim strips down to his boxers and Jeff and Chip take his clothes and run over a small bridge that takes them to the other side. Anthony, Johnny, and I are in hysterics.

Jim jumps in cannonball style and makes a huge splash, yelling something that sounds like, "Bombs away!" I can hear a few animated Italian voices in the distance, nearby onlookers cheering him on. Jim manages to dog paddle his way across the filthy canal in comical fashion as more and more people line up to egg him on. He crosses to a thunderous ovation.

"Take that Europe!" I hear Jim roar from across the other side, his beer gut wobbling as he pumps his fist in the air. "America!"

"I think that's enough for one evening," says Anthony.

"Yeah, me too," says Johnny.

"I could use a coffee," I say. "Let's bail."

THE KILLING MOON

On the way to Rome we stop in Florence for three days. Anthony seems to enjoy it the most and even takes an overnight excursion to see the Leaning Tower of Pisa, which isn't too far away. Johnny and I pass. I dig the architecture, cafés, and women, but Johnny is pretty nervous about getting to Rome and seeing Sophia and the tension is rubbing off on me. Time and distance has helped me forget about Julie and Christine, but I still need to get my shit together and make a decision about next year. My parents might not want me to stay at Essex, but I've decided not to kowtow to their wishes and return to Ann Arbor. New York feels like the best option. If I can find a job there I won't be dependent on them for money. This feels like the path of least resistance.

Johnny and I spend the afternoon checking out a few sites, but mostly just laze about and drink too much coffee. In the evening we decide to go out for drinks and maybe even find a club. We've been seeing way too many grownups in cafés and wine bars, time to try to find the kids and see if they're alright. We don't know where we're going as we walk along the dark Florence streets, relying on instinct rather than common sense, or even a street map. We see a goth couple in the distance. They look like they could be catwalk models. The guy is tall and thin, at least 6' 3" and has slicked back black hair like Dave Vanian from The Damned. He's wearing a frilly white shirt, a long black cape, skinny black trousers, and black boots. The girl is very tall and thin, too, pale with long flowing black hair, looking stunning in a designer black dress and dominatrix boots.

"Hey, let's shadow them and see what they're up to," says Johnny.

"Are we Starsky and Hutch, now?

"I call Hutch," says Johnny.

"Then, I call Harry Callahan. I don't like Starsky."

Johnny laughs. "I don't like Starsky either."

We're being silly, but it seems like a good plan. Of course, we could just be friendly and actually talk to the Italian goths, but we're having more fun playing detective. The couple veers off on to a little cobblestone side street, where we can see some more goths and stylish punks milling about. There must be a club nearby. The two of us are dressed reasonably well: Johnny is wearing a black Merc jacket with a white Ben Sherman button down and I'm wearing a black button down with my black leather jacket. We see the couple and their friends enter through an unmarked door.

"I don't see a sign anywhere," says Johnny. "Think this place is legit?"

"Who knows? It has to be a club or a private party. What's the worst that could happen?" I ask.

"I don't know... human sacrifice? Maybe we'll get drugged and someone will steal our kidneys."

We both laugh and I open the door. At least it's not green. We head down a spiral staircase and it suddenly gets very dark with just a few flickers of red light guiding our way. We can hear The Dance Society's version of The Rolling Stones' "2000 Light Years From Home" coming from somewhere down below. Dracula's lair? At the bottom of the staircase we find ourselves in a tricked out subterranean club. It's not a dive like the basement at Essex. We see people lounging on black and red leather couches, while others are dancing up a storm as a stern, serious looking DJ with spiky bleached blonde hair thumbs through stacks of vinyl. Behind the DJ is a projection of the classic Max Schreck vampire flick *Nosferatu*. To the left of the DJ booth and dance floor is a long black metallic bar. Above the bar there's a small red neon sign that simply says, "Inferno." We're greeted by a bouncer who looks much too big to be wearing leather pants and a tight mesh t-shirt. We don't tell him that. He asks for identification and the two of us display our passports.

"Ah, Americanos. Christian Death, 45 Grave," he says, hoping we'll recognize the obscure American goth groups.

"Right on, brother," says Johnny.

I know for a fact that Johnny doesn't dig the goth scene, but he can be a charmer, which helps in potentially volatile situations like this one.

"Danse Society, nice," Johnny continues, giving the thumbs up to our intense but friendly bouncer.

The bouncer clasps our backs and says, "Welcome, Americanos."

We walk to the bar and order a couple of glasses of house red. Red wine seems to be the drink of choice here. At least I hope they're drinking wine. The two of us walk over to an empty couch and soak in the atmosphere. It's a pretty fascinating place. For one thing, the girls are smoking hot. They're not as heavily made up as their English and American goth sisters, leaning much more to the sexy rather than scary side of the subculture—lots of visible cleavage and skintight leather. A lot of the guys are wearing leather too.

"I'm pretty open-minded, but I don't know about dudes in leather pants, especially that guy," says Johnny pointing to a man in bottomless chaps.

"Men shouldn't wear leather pants unless they're Iggy Pop," I say in agreement.

"Or Jim Morrison before he got fat," says Johnny.

The music is incredible. We hear Sisters of Mercy, Red Lorry Yellow Lorry, Siouxsie and The Banshees, and, of course, Bauhaus.

"This DJ is fucking good," I say. "The crowd's worshiping him like he's Italian Bono or something."

He's killing me softly with his songs. I feel envious of the power he has over the crowd. In another life, on another coast, I will experience a similar thrill, but right now the thought of manning the decks anywhere seems preposterous.

"I've DJed before," says Johnny.

"No shit?!"

"Yeah, I had a show on WNYU where I would play a lot of mod and 2-Tone. I've spun at a few parties, too."

Johnny keeps getting cooler and cooler in my book.

The DJ follows "Bela Lugosi's Dead" with an extended remix of "The Killing Moon."

"Shit," I say with awe. "This has to be one of the best songs ever. This DJ is ace. He's playing all the goth Motown."

Johnny laughs. "What the fuck is goth Motown?"

I try to explain. The term just came to me out of nowhere. "You know, all the hits. Everything on Motown is so great and timeless. These are the goth equivalents."

"I like it, man," says Johnny, "but don't tell Spicoli!"

"Yeah, no more Beatles and Motown!"

"I dig the Bunnymen," says Johnny, "but this song just makes me sad."

"Me, too. I used to play this album with Christine a lot."

"I feel like the guy in the song is so helpless. It's like he knows his life is about to get fucked, but he's just standing his ground and facing the music."

"I never thought about it that way. That whole 'fate up against your will' line kills me though. Weirdly enough I flashed back to that line when I kissed Julie for the first time. Wonder if that was some kind of omen?"

"Do you believe in fate?" Johnny asks.

"I don't know. Sometimes I do, but other times I know it's my own fucking fault when shit goes wrong."

"I think I'm with you on that, but crap like love and romance seems so heavy sometimes. This whole thing with Sophia is wearing me down. I feel like I have a week to figure it out and get it right or else it might never work."

"Yeah, that's deep, man. You know I've got my fingers crossed for you. You're about the best friend I've ever had. Sorry if I'm sounding all gay."

Johnny laughs. "Ditto, you're a good dude, Drew.

You'll find someone better than Julie. I guarantee it."

"I hope so, man."

The DJ seems to realize that "The Killing Moon," as beautiful and epic of a song as it might be, isn't exactly floor filler material and follows with Dead or Alive's campy smash hit "You Spin Me Round (Like A Record)" and Doctor and The Medic's equally preposterous cover of the hippie anthem "Spirit In The Sky." The Italian goths eat it up and storm the dance floor like it's the Bastille.

We lock eyes with a group of girls.

Johnny signals to me and says, "*Let's Dance.*"

ROMAN HOLIDAY

We're finally in Rome. Sophia is even more beautiful in real life than in the photos Johnny has showed me. She's tall, thin and very stylish, the perfect female counterpart to Johnny. They look like they belong together, a rock star and a model. Sophia's no dumb brunette though. She's finishing up at the University of Rome soon, an honor student specializing in Romance languages. Johnny, Anthony, and I score a ground level room in a low end pensione with a decent weekly rate. It's cold and damp with virtually nonexistent heat, but at least we have our own bathroom.

Sophia has a lot of stuff planned and over the first three days we get the royal treatment, visiting a lot of the famous sites, like the Coliseum, Circus Maximus, Catacombs, Spanish Steps, Trevi Fountain, and the Vatican City. She navigates her black Audi through the narrow, winding Roman streets as if she were a Formula One driver, a favorite mix tape on constant loop. Years from now I will associate "Up On The Catwalk" and "The Killing Moon" with this trip, so engrained that youthful imprint has become.

I'm feeling like Iggy Pop's "Passenger," only Rome is my Berlin, but I can tell that Johnny is getting agitated. On almost every outing, Sophia invites along friends and I can sense that Johnny is dying for some alone time. He doesn't say anything to me, or act up in any way, but I've known him long enough that I can pick up on his moods. Those frustrations aside, I like Sophia's friends. There's a hot looking girl named Monica with curves like a porn star—Anthony and I try not to stare at her too much (Johnny seems oblivious)—and two guys, who always seem to tag along: Stefano, who is dating Claudia, and Marcello, who at times seems to be a tad too friendly with Sophia. Stefano and Marcello are both very nice and like most Italian guys, they're pretty stylish in a GQ kind of way. They favor skinny jeans and Gucci loafers, worn with v-necks or silky shirts, obligatory two or three buttons undone.

On our fourth evening in Rome, our group has a fun night out that includes a stroll through some out of the way side streets. Afterward we all hang out at Stefano and Marcello's pad, drinking coffee and watching an Italian music video channel, their version of MTV, but even better. I feel like jumping up and screaming like a schoolgirl when "Just Like Honey" comes on.

"You like them, yes?" says buxom Claudia, who looks like she might explode out of her sleeveless black top.

"My favorite band!"

"Yeah, he listens to them all the time on his Walkman," complains Anthony.

"I'm that loud?"

"Ha, yeah," says Johnny, "but I dig the tunes."

Johnny seems to be in a better mood. I saw him spend some time with Sophia in the kitchen while she was preparing coffee for everyone. In a way it's a pretty good omen that the three of us have had constant company in Rome even though Johnny might say otherwise. The day we arrived, the U.S. bombed Libya in retaliation for a nightclub bombing in West Berlin that had been conducted by Libyan agents ten days prior. There's been a lot of anti-American sentiment in the newspapers and on the streets. Johnny and I joke that maybe we should pretend to be Canadians for the duration of our trip and start saying "eh" a lot. Anthony won't have any of this and we get into arguments with him over the situation and American foreign policy in general.

"All this crap wouldn't happen if America just minded their own fucking business," Johnny exclaims when we get home from the Gucci brothers (Johnny's nickname for

Stefano and Marcello) apartment and crash out in the dungeon, our collective pet name for our dank place of residency.

"No way," says Anthony. "If America didn't do anything we'd be overrun with Communists."

"What, like fucking *Red Dawn*?" I say.

Johnny laughs.

"Not quite," says Anthony stuttering a bit, "but the Communists are a threat and they're in allegiance with all of the evil terrorist organizations around the world."

"Except for the ones we're in allegiance with," dead pans Johnny.

"Like who?" asks Anthony.

"I don't know, the Contras in Nicaragua are a start," says Johnny.

"They're freedom fighters," Anthony says.

"Let's just agree to disagree, man," says Johnny. He's not one to stay angry for too long. "I'm very pissed off about the bombing, but truth be told, I've been pretty pissed off about Sophia, too.

"What can we do?" I ask.

"Yeah, if you want us to get lost so you can spend time with her, I'm cool with that," says Anthony.

"It's not you guys that are the problem," says Johnny. "I can't make out what the deal is with Marcello. I asked her about him in the kitchen tonight and she was like, 'don't be silly Johnny, he's just a friend,' but I don't know. I feel like this is over my head. What Drew went through at Essex has put me on pins and needles. She says we'll talk soon, whatever that fucking means."

"Christ, don't remind me."

"I'm hardly a ladies' man," says Anthony, "but I feel like if something is meant to be right, it should feel right. You should know. It shouldn't feel like a struggle. Maybe I've just read too much and experienced too little..."

"No, you're fucking right," says Johnny. "I've hung on to girls way past their sell by date, even when I knew it wasn't right, easy to get in, hard to get out."

"I wish some girls were easier to get in," I say.

Everyone laughs. Anthony's right. Life shouldn't feel like a fucking struggle all the time. Everyone has their passions, but more often than not they get sidetracked. My dad and Paul are lucky because they both knew they wanted to be professors from day one. Other guys like that Spicoli dude we met in Camden seem to be the opposite, taking life one day at a time.

BEVERLY HILLS PUNK

Anthony has been fretting about school, panicking about falling further behind on his work, even though it's vacation, and the next day, very abruptly, decides to leave for Essex—as in right now. Meanwhile, Johnny's wish has come true. He returns from a payphone in an ecstatic mood. He called Sophia to see what the agenda was for the day and she invited him to spend a couple of nights with her at a country villa her family owns outside of Rome. They're leaving tonight.

"Shit, Drew, I don't mean to put you out like that."

"Yeah, I feel really bad, now," says Anthony, "but I really need to get back. I've been freaking out about my essays."

"No worries, man," I say. "You're too young to get an ulcer, Anthony. Do what you have to do."

After Anthony packs up and leaves, Johnny and I get coffee at a place around the corner and I can tell that Johnny still feels bad about leaving me alone.

"Shit, Johnny, you need to figure out what's going on with Sophia. This is your perfect chance to get it right… "

"…or wrong."

"Try to stay positive. I know that probably sounds funny coming from me, but I mean it. Do you think she'd really move to New York to be with you?"

"That's what I need to find out. We talked about it in Spain, but it's kind of become a taboo subject lately. She just keeps on saying maybe. I hope I can convince her. I'd stay in Italy, but what would I do here without a degree? Besides my band would fucking kill me."

"Do you love her?"

"I think I do, man."

The look on Johnny's face convinces me that he'd take a bullet for her.

That evening I do nothing other than read over-priced copies of *Rolling Stone* and *Spin* that I purchased from a nearby newsstand. The three-week European adventure has finally caught up with me. After reading the magazines, I flip through a recent issue of *The Village Voice* that one of Johnny's friends mailed to him. I stumble across an ad for a 1-900 bondage fetish hotline with a strangely familiar photo. On closer inspection, I realize that it's the exact same image that Christine sent to me at Christmas, the one with her decked out in leather, fishnets, and dominatrix boots, whip in hand. She's obviously become a fetish model and god knows what else? This certainly explains why she could always afford so many records on a retail salary. I cringe, thinking about what else she might end up doing when she moves to L.A.

I hit the sack at around 9:00pm and manage to sleep for close to eleven hours straight. Not used to being up so early, I decide that I might as well make a full day of it. Johnny won't be back until the next morning, and a few hours after that, the two of us will head back to Essex. I shower and feel like dressing a little nice for a change. My white button down is pretty creased so I hang it in the bathroom while I let the hot shower blast for about ten minutes—ghetto dry cleaning. Johnny told me about that trick one day when I asked him how he's managed to keep his shirts so wrinkle free on this trip.

I opt for jeans, DM's, and borrow Johnny's suit jacket. I'm at peace with the decision I made last night. I've decided to go to New York in the fall. I'll fly back to Ann Arbor in June after my last exam at Essex, work for a few months to save some money, and then head to the Big Apple in September or October. I need at least a semester off to clear my head. I called my parents, yesterday, to tell them this. They were strangely OK. I think once I told them that Julie and I had broken up, I was able to garner some sympathy.

My mom kept asking if I was OK and suggested that maybe I should speak to a counselor to work out my feelings. I assured her I was fine, but just needed a little space, telling her that New York was what I needed right now.

"I need to see if I like it before moving there for a potential writing job after I graduate," I said, giving them enough assurance that I planned on going back to school, even though at this moment I feel undecided.

She looks like Bardot in the movies or that famous picture of her on the bicycle. She's tall, probably just a few inches shorter than me with long straight blonde hair and is wearing a simple, yet timeless black sleeveless dress (probably Chanel or something), and a pair of big expensive looking aviator shades. She's walking out of the neighborhood café near the Trevi Fountain that Johnny and I have been frequenting on a regular basis. She sits down at one of the small round tables outside and removes her sunglasses, revealing dazzling blue eyes. I wonder if she's a model killing time before a shoot, or, perhaps, even an actress. She pulls out one of those colorful user friendly maps that all the tourists seem to favor and opens it up. As I begin to enter the café, she signals to me.

"*Buongiorno*," she says in an American accent. "*Dove Spanish Steps?*"

I laugh.

"I speak English. I can show you how to get there in a second. Mind if I grab a cup of coffee, first? I can't think without caffeine."

"Sure," she says with a smile. She looks even more radiant. "I have all the time in the world today."

"Me, too. I'll be right back."

I try to regain some composure. Jesus is she beautiful.

I get my coffee and sit opposite her. I half expected her to be gone as if I were having an amazing dream that just went south as the alarm clock buzzed, but she's still there.

"Hi again," I say. "I'm Drew by the way."

"I'm Vanessa."

She takes my hand. Her skin feels so soft and smooth that it takes a concentrated effort to let go.

"Where are you from Drew?"

"Ann Arbor, originally, but I'm in England now for my junior year abroad. I'm at the University of Essex in Colchester."

"That sounds fun. I've been to London, but not anywhere else in England. I've been almost everywhere in Europe though."

"Where are you from?" I ask. I'm guessing New York City or L.A. She's too cool to be from anywhere else.

"L.A. Well, Beverly Hills," she says with a sheepish grin, perhaps not sure how I might feel about someone from a filthy rich enclave.

"Cool. I've never been to L.A. I've always wanted to go." Right now I want to go there more than anything in the world.

"It's pretty great. I have no complaints."

"What are you doing in Rome?" I ask. "Are you studying abroad this year?"

"No, I'm here with my mom. They're making a movie out of one of her novels. She's off in the countryside somewhere until tomorrow afternoon. I'm home alone today, woe is me."

I ask who her mom is. She mentions the name of a woman whose period piece romance novels can be found anywhere in the world, from the finest bookstores to tiny newsstands and airport kiosks. She's massive. Even my mom has read some of those books. No wonder Vanessa's from Beverly Hills. How couldn't she be?

"So how long are you going to be in Rome?" I ask.

"Just for a few more days. I have to be back in school next Monday."

"Where do you go to school?"

"Beverly Hills High School."

Crap, I think to myself. My supermodel dream girl has suddenly turned into jail bait. Maybe she's eighteen.

"You look older. I mean that it in a good way," I say, hoping she'll take it as a compliment.

"I get that a lot," she laughs. "I'm only sixteen."

OK, I say to myself, this conversation has officially turned platonic.

Vanessa asks me what I'm doing in Rome and I tell her about the last three weeks and the saga of Johnny and Sophia.

"That sounds like something my mom would like to write about; a tall, dark and handsome American and a beautiful Italian girl," she says with a smile. She mimics one of those movie preview voices and giggles, "Will the young lovers find happiness or will they be doomed like Romeo and Juliet?"

Vanessa finally sounds like a kid, but she's perfect. I wish I could freeze myself for about five years and meet her in the future.

"So do you have any plans today?" she asks.

"No, nothing at all."

"Then let's have a *Roman Holiday.*"

I'm impressed that she knows the Audrey Hepburn and Cary Grant film. I'm not much of a film buff, but I do know a lot of the classics from when my parents would take me and Paul to the art house theaters in Ann Arbor that showed all the old black and white flicks.

We start walking toward the Spanish Steps.

"So what do you like to do, Drew?"

I notice that some coffee is still on the side of her mouth, so I gesture to her by running my finger alongside my mouth. She wipes off the coffee with her index finger and briefly licks on it. Maybe for a little too long I think or maybe my mind is just playing tricks on me. This is just what I need; Lolita from Beverly Hills on my last day in Rome. Her mom's famous enough that I might actually make a tabloid or two.

"I like music," I say, trying to keep my thoughts above the waistline. "I'm hoping to get a job with a magazine when I graduate."

"That's really cool. Who are your favorite bands?"

I list some of my usual suspects and throw in a few of the new groups that I've discovered this year, like Primal Scream and Spacemen 3.

"What about you?" I ask.

"I really like The Church. I listen to *Heyday* all the time when I paint. And I like Simple Minds and Roxy Music and Depeche Mode... I really love Depeche Mode."

"You've got really great taste."

"Thanks. I actually used to be a total punk until about a year ago."

"No way, you don't look it at all."

She lifts up her hair and shows me formerly shaved sections above her ears that are now in the process of growing out.

"I used to have liberty spikes. It was fun for awhile, but I got sick of that whole scene. I had this boyfriend who was totally like a vegan and he'd always freak out about germs and stuff. It got so annoying. He was like twenty-four and he still lived with his parents. What a loser."

Christ. This girl's grown up fast; jet setting around the world and going out with guys much older than her. Suddenly, I feel young at twenty-one, but not young enough for her.

"So are you an artist?" I ask.

"Definitely, though I don't know if I want to go into painting or animation, maybe both. I want to go to art school for sure. I'm pretty bad at all of my classes except English. I can't imagine going to a normal college."

"I was like that, too. My dad's a professor and my brother is about to become one. My mom's an editor."

"My dad was a producer. He died when I was just a kid."

"I'm really sorry," I say.

"It's OK. I didn't know him too well, but I miss the idea of having a dad. My mom has a bunch of dumb boyfriends. She's too busy to make anything work."

"Do you have any siblings?" I ask.

"No, it's just me."

"That must be lonely."

"Sometimes it is, but I like to be alone. I paint a lot and listen to music and watch a lot of old movies. I tend to like anything that's black and white. Do you like Joan Crawford?"

"I only know who she is."

"We must see a Joan Crawford movie together someday. We really must."

I don't say anything. She's acting like the two of us have all the time in the world, but in less than a day Johnny and I will be heading back to Essex.

We get to the Spanish Steps and Vanessa grabs my hand and says, "Let's run to the top."

We race up the steep steps hand-in-hand and are pretty breathless when we reach the pinnacle.

Vanessa wants ice cream even though it's not yet lunchtime (*god, she's so cool*), so the two of us stop for gelato at a sidewalk café. My mind flashes back to that Sunday in March when Dave, Julie, Claire, and I had 99's in Clacton. Just a month ago Julie and Dave were two of my dearest friends on the planet. Now I hope to never see them again. I know I'll be able to avoid Julie to some extent, since she lives in Colchester and we don't have any classes together, but I'll have to confront Dave. I wonder what Claire's been up to. She was a lot of fun, but probably hates me now. Julie's no doubt poisoned her against me.

"So where are you staying in Rome?" I ask.

"We're at The Excelsior. My mom has expensive tastes."

"I'd say. Do you run up room service while she's away?"

"Sometimes," she responds with a mischievous grin. "I've been pretty good though. Every day I make sure to do something cultural like see a museum or a tourist attraction. Or just walk. Like today I got up real early for a change and I found you."

"Hope I'm not a disappointment."

"No, not at all. In fact, I've decided that you're mine for the day. I want to buy you dinner at the hotel tonight to thank you for being such a good guide."

"It's a date. Anything else you want to do?"

"Have you been to any good record stores here? I need to buy some new tapes for my flight back or I'll just die."

"I can help you with that."

Sophia had taken Johnny and I to a hip little independent shop called Transmission that I'm sure Vanessa would dig. The two of us set off in search of a phone book to track down the address.

We spend a few hours at Transmission just looking at all the vinyl, even though neither of us has access to a turntable right now.

"I love album art when it's done right," she says. "Cassettes are easy to listen to but they're pretty disposable. My mom just bought a CD player, can you believe that?"

"Wow, no shit. Those are expensive. My brother Paul has one. His wife is a lawyer so they have a lot of bread. He says that once you listen to music on CD you'll never want to go back. He loves classical though. Rock 'n' roll isn't really supposed to sound nice and clean."

"For sure. So what should I buy for my trip home?"

I like that she's looking up to me. She buys *Psychocandy*, *Sparkle In The Rain*, and the new *Catching Up With Depeche Mode* best-of, even though she already has all of their albums.

"It has a new version of 'Fly On The Windscreen,'" she says, justifying her purchase. I like her zeal.

"Are you getting anything, Drew?"

"I wish, but I'm a bit tight on funds until I get back to England. I need to start saving a bit, too, if I'm going to move to New York in the fall."

I tell her about my plans to take some time off of school and she tells me how much she loves it in New York City.

"You'll have to keep in touch," she says. "I might come visit you some time."

"That would be nice."

"Let me buy you something, Drew."

"It's OK. You really don't have to."

But she does. She buys me the vinyl of *Psychocandy*, telling me that it's an early house warming present for my new place in New York.

It's almost dinnertime and we cab it back to the Excelsior. Vanessa has a huge wad of cash and pays the cabbie before I have a chance to offer. Money obviously isn't an issue to her. Vanessa's going to make someone the happiest man on earth. She's so smart, beautiful, funny, with perfect taste in the arts, and being filthy rich doesn't hurt.

I'm not too jealous though. I know Vanessa's too young for me and that we're just having fun today, but it does hit home that I have more in common with her, a random sixteen year old girl, who I just met, than I ever did with Christine or Julie. Christine liked all the same music that I did, but outside of that we had nothing in common other than sexual compatibility for a brief moment in time. Julie was twenty going on forty. I'm not sure if it's because of her working class roots, but she was in too much of a hurry to grow up and settle down. Having a lot of fun wasn't really an option. I can afford to screw around for a while and find myself and that's what I'm going to do.

I don't want to know how much the dinner cost. Vanessa just charges it to her mom's suite. I feel like I'm on an episode of *Lifestyles of the Rich and Famous*. We have a multiple course dinner with a nice bottle of red—Vanessa keeps ordering different things for us to sample, not bothered if we finish it or not. I feel like a food critic given full reign of the menu. My favorites are the ravioli with a shrimp sauce and a super lean beef filet, but everything I try is amazing. For desert we have crème brulet and port.

I walk her to her suite to say good night. Her mom has a huge master bedroom done Baroque style that looks big enough to fit a basketball court inside, while Vanessa has a smaller room to herself, which dwarves the size of our pensione dungeon. I tell her so.

"I think that sounds romantic. The three of you slumming across Europe like *On The Road*. My mom is really overprotective. I love her, but I can't wait to get out."

"Trust me, you don't want to stay in that dive. I'm all for slumming, but that place has tested my limits."

"Would you like to stay and watch a movie with me?" she asks.

"Sure, if you're not sick of me yet."

She laughs and says, "Not at all."

We sit on her bed and watch this dumb Seventies Italian action flick, amusing ourselves by making up dialogue. Just before I leave she goes to the desk and jots something down on a piece of stationery. She hands it to me. It's her address and phone number.

"In case you're ever in L.A.," she says.

"Thanks."

I give her my parents' address and number for the time being and tell her I'll write when I get to New York.

"We can be pen pals," she says. "That will be fun."

We hug and she gives me a quick peck on the lips.

"It was really great meeting you, Drew."

"Likewise, Vanessa."

I don't feel like taking a cab. It's too nice of an evening. The pensione is about a half hour walk from the Excelsior so I hoof it on foot. I stop at the Trevi Fountain. It's getting close to midnight and it's still all lit up. There aren't too many tourists around now so I'm able to find a perfect spot to sit, soak in the vibes, and admire the amazing marble art. Back in the day everyone seemed to be much more patient. Artists would take years working on commissions, be it paintings or sculptures like the ones around me. Now everything feels so fast paced and disposable, even art. For every great record I'm rewarded with, I feel like I have to be subjected to an endless array of disposable MTV garbage in return. Johnny and I were at the fountain just the other day and a group of four schoolgirls asked if they could take our photo. From what Johnny could make out via his passable Spanish was that the girls seemed truly convinced that we were famous musicians. We didn't try to dissuade them at all.

Hopefully everything has gone well with Johnny and Sophia. Anthony's probably almost back at Essex by now, no doubt chomping at the bit to get started on homework again. I wonder if I'll ever become that driven or if I'll be more like Spicoli when I'm old. I haven't felt this peaceful in a long time, certainly not since I split up with Julie. The Italians have it right. Everyone seems much more relaxed here. This place is good for my soul. I toss a coin into the fountain and give thanks for the nice day I had before heading back.

When Johnny arrives in the morning I can tell things didn't go well. He mumbles a quick greeting and says he really needs to take a shower. After he cleans up we walk over to our favorite café.

"We'll never be anything more than friends," says Johnny.

"Shit, I'm sorry man."

"It's no one's fault. I can tell how much she loves Rome and her family and friends here. I can't pull her away from that, and I can't come here. New York's part of my soul—I could never leave."

"Damn. I'm so sad. I was really pulling for you. I'm a sucker for romantic stories like that. I hope you at least had some fun at the villa."

"We most definitely did. The countryside is pretty surreal and just because we may only be friends doesn't mean I was totally celibate if you catch my drift."

"Ha! At least you have something nice to remember her by."

"What about you Drew? Hope your day wasn't too boring."

"Dude, you're not going to believe me."

I tell him about Vanessa.

"Christ, you should move to L.A. and patiently wait until she turns eighteen," says Johnny.

"So I made up my mind to come to New York in the fall," I say, changing the subject.

"Holy shit, Drew. That's the best news I've heard in a long time. We can room together, now that Sophia won't be coming."

"Awesome. I'm really looking forward to that."

"Me, too."

The train ride is relentlessly long, but we have a lot of fun. Johnny tells me stories about all his favorite clubs and hangouts in New York and, suddenly, September seems too far away. I've had enough of England.

When we arrive in London, Johnny says, "Fuck it, let's find a McDonald's to celebrate your move to New York. I'm tired of all this English crap like soggy chips and vinegar. I'm fucking starving."

We get off at Oxford Circle and, immediately, find a Micky D's. We scarf down our food like a couple of competitive eaters, attracting some disapproving looks from a stern British family nearby. Fuck it, I think, it's OK to be an ugly American once in awhile.

VELOCITY GIRL

It's almost May and I've been back at Essex for a week now. Tension is in the air as everyone around me is getting worked up into a mad state as they prepare for final exams in five weeks. The procrastinators are freaking out as they try to condense a year's worth of little to no work into a few weeks of cramming, while the studious, like Anthony, are licking their chops, ready to show off their A-game. I fall somewhere in between. My head is in New York, but I don't want this year to be a total waste either, so I hit the books with a flourish that surprises me.

It helps that I no longer have many outside distractions. I've been avoiding the Union Bar like the plague since I no longer hang out with Dave, and, by default, his crowd. Johnny's been bummed out by the whole Sophia experience, and while the two of us still see each other to shoot the shit about what we'll be doing in New York in the fall, he's been hiding away a lot in his room, banging out new songs on an acoustic that he rented from a guitar shop in Colchester. Both of our heads seem to have left England.

I'm in my room, trying to make sense out of *Das Kapital* when I hear a knock on the door.

"Oi, Drew. It's Dave."

"What the fuck do you want?"

I haven't talked to him since the episode with Julie. I walk to the door, open it, and eye him up as if we're about to engage in a duel. Ten steps back gents and raise your pistols.

"A telegram just came for you."

He hands it to me.

"Look Drew, I'm really sorry about Julie. I fucked up. I know you won't forgive me, but I wanted to let you know that I'm sorry."

I don't respond.

"Look, I'm just sorry," he says again. Suddenly, the whole thing just seems trivial. I'm going to New York. Fuck England.

"We'll always have Manchester," I call out to him as he walks down the hall.

"That we will," he says, slowly turning his head back to me.

The telegram is from my mom. It just says, "Call us as soon as you can."

I call from one of the payphones in the square. PJ's dead. My mom tells me that he crashed his car into a tree going twice the speed limit on the winding Huron River Drive, a scenic road I ran thousands of miles on as a kid. He had cocaine and alcohol in his system.

"Christ," I say. That's all I can muster.

"I'm sorry," replies my mom. "I know you two used to be close in high school and that you had become friends again."

"We stopped hanging out last summer. I don't even remember the last time I talked to him."

Of course, I'm lying. I remember well. PJ, Danny, and I were all coked up and painting Ypsilanti red. That's my last memory of him. It suddenly hits me that we could have all just as easily been in a car crash that night. I doubt PJ was any higher when he died than he was that evening. I'm too choked up to talk any more so I tell my mom I'll call her next week.

I get off the phone feeling dazed, stunned, and a little pissed off. What a fucking waste. I want to get drunk, but decide against it. I feel too depressed and lonely, even for that. I start walking back to the flat, holding back tears, and run into Claire, who's heading in the opposite direction.

"Hello, Drew. How are you? Is everything OK? You look terrible if you don't mind me saying so."

Claire certainly doesn't look terrible. In fact, she looks really stylish, even in casual mode; black skirt, Cure t-shirt, low top black Chuck Taylors with pink shoelaces.

I tell her about PJ.

"Drew, I'm so sorry," she says. "What a terrible shock. Let's go back to my flat. I'll make you some tea."

"Are you sure? I don't want to interrupt any plans."

"The library can wait. Let's get you sorted out."

We sit in the kitchen and I tell Claire about some of my European adventures with Johnny until the kettle boils. Afterward we go to her room. I take a seat on the edge of her bed and she sits next to me and, suddenly, hugs me. I wasn't expecting that.

I tell Claire about PJ. How we used to be close and how we drifted apart over the summer, other than that last wild cocaine-fueled night we spent with Danny.

"Something similar happened to me when I was younger, although we weren't on good terms when she died," Claire tells me. "When I was thirteen I had a silly fight with my best friend in school, Alison. It was over some boy we both liked. A week later she was killed with some others in an IRA bombing at a department store. I still think about it all the time."

"Jesus, now I feel really awful. I've made you feel bad. I'm a real mess today."

"It's OK. I'm glad you came by. I really am."

Claire seems to be struggling to say something more.

"This will cheer us up," she says, changing the subject.

She takes a cassette from her shelf and hands it to me.

"It's a compilation I just ordered from the *NME*," she says.

The cassette says C86 on the cover. It's a collection of new bands that *NME* thinks will go places this year. I immediately notice that the first track is Primal Scream "Velocity Girl," the song that blew me away so much way when I saw them play in Camden with Nick. I insert the cassette into her boombox and it sounds even more majestic than I remember.

"I saw Primal Scream back in November," I tell her. "They played with Meat Whiplash. It was a great show."

"I wish you had taken me," says Claire.

"I don't think we even knew each other then."

"Ah, your memory is hazier than mine. I always used to notice you at the Union Bar with Dave and his lot, and then there was that night when the two of you did the Wiv Run and you tried to dance with us."

"I do remember that. Not one of my finer moments."

"You were wearing a Psychedelic Furs t-shirt and I saw you walking towards us. I kept hoping you wanted to talk to me. I thought you were really cute that night, even if you were pissed."

She laughs before continuing.

"But you asked Julie to dance, and then at the Jesus and Mary Chain show when I had you alone, you asked me about her again."

"God, I'm so sorry. I'm such an idiot. You can see I learned my lesson."

The right girl had been under my nose the whole damn time I've been here.

"I'm so sorry, Drew. How awful of me. I never even told you how sorry I am about Julie. We actually had a little fight over you."

"So what happened?" I ask. This is intriguing.

"Julie told me that she had gone through your stuff. It was right after that Clacton trip. She had it in her head that you were hiding something, so she searched through your things and found a notebook that had some entries about a girl called Christine..."

"That's so over," I interrupt.

Claire laughs. "No need to be so defensive. I believe you! My point is that I told Julie that it was none of her business what you wrote and to just leave it alone. She expected my sympathy when you wouldn't forgive her about Dave."

"Don't remind me of that dirt bag."

"Sorry. Dave's a bloody wanker. I'm really sorry, poor

you."

She puts her hand on my shoulder.

"My, you two are looking cozy," comes a voice from the door.

Claire and I look up. It's Julie. I had left the door open when we went into Claire's room. God knows how long Julie has been standing there.

"I was going to see if you wanted to go over some notes for our Shakespeare exam, Claire," says Julie, "but I see you already have everything you need."

She turns abruptly and stomps out.

"I better chase her down," says Claire, looking me in the eye. "Don't be a stranger."

"I won't, Claire."

I go back to my room and put on The Violent Femmes album, PJ's favorite record, trying to think of better days. I take two shots of Jack, one for me and one for PJ, and sit back in bed, thinking of things I wish I'd said.

As a kid, PJ was the best little league baseball player in town, a stud pitcher with a colossal batting average to boot. His teams would always beat ours. He went to a different junior high than I did, but by the time seventh grade rolled around, he was pretty legendary. Everyone knew who he was. All the girls had crushes on him and I'm certain I wasn't the only guy who wanted to be like him. Back then he had long feathered hair—kind of like Scott Baio—and wore a puka shell necklace. I heard rumors that he had finger banged a girl before I even knew what that meant. We formally met in eighth grade. In addition to his baseball prowess, he was a star runner, winning the city meet in the 400 and the 800. I won the mile that day, only because he didn't run it. After my race he congratulated me and suggested that we train together that summer since we were both going to start freshman year at the same high school.

"We're the two fastest dudes in the city for our age, man," he said. "We ought to stick together."

And just like that we became inseparable. Every

morning we'd run for an hour and then chill at his place drinking cokes, eating Chips Ahoy! cookies, and shooting the shit. Sometimes we'd ride bikes to visit girls he knew. Being seen with PJ raised my social status significantly. Other times we'd just listen to music. Back then live albums were all the rage. My old friends and I would kick out the jams to *Frampton Comes Alive!* and the two Kiss *Alive* albums, but PJ upped the ante. He had Cheap Trick *At Budokan.*

One day we were lifting weights in his basement with "Surrender" blasting on the stereo, when his older brother, who was home from college for the summer, called us fags for listening to Cheap Trick. He told us we needed to listen to *Never Mind The Bollocks* and that's how I first heard punk. The music sounded so raw and impossible that it actually scared me until a few years later when Richie introduced me to The Stooges. After getting into The Stooges, the Sex Pistols were pure bubblegum, but in junior high, man, they were downright terrifying.

PJ also turned me on to alcohol. He was old for our grade, turning sixteen in September of our sophomore year, so he got his license months before the rest of us. One night we watched *The Warriors* at an art house theatre on the University of Michigan campus. A few minutes into the picture, just after Riffs gang leader, Cyrus, got shot, PJ reached into his coat pocket and handed me a can of Schlitz. He had liberated a six pack from his dad's beer fridge and strategically placed the cans in various pockets of his parka. These days I'd puke after a few sips of Schlitz, but back then I felt like a true juvenile delinquent, sipping contraband beer, while watching a flick, which back then required parental permission for kids under eighteen.

The Violent Femmes cassette ends and I can hear my neighbor's stereo from below—Fine Young Cannibals "Johnny Come Home." Roland Gift is asking the world what is so wrong with his life that he must get drunk every night, and I wonder the same thing before taking another swig of whiskey.

WIVENHOE REVISITED

It's the following afternoon and I'm in the library. I've finished taking notes from a book about Trotsky for my political violence class and I'm returning it to its rightful place on the shelf. My mind's in a fog and I run smack into Claire, knocking her books and papers out of her hands. This is the second time in two days that I've literally run into her.

"Fancy meeting you here," she laughs as she picks up her things. "I didn't realize you even knew what a library was."

"I'm not that bad. Really, I'm not." I'm a little embarrassed that she thinks I'm that much of a slacker.

"I'm just teasing you," she says.

She looks fantastic in DM's and a tight black tank top.

"Are you doing anything right now?" I ask.

"I was going to work on an essay, but if you have a better offer, I'm all ears."

"Let's get out of here, then. Do you feel like getting a coffee or something?"

"I'd love to."

She's smiling as if I told her she won the lottery.

"There's a nice little spot in Wivenhoe if you don't mind a little walk," she says.

"No, not at all."

We leave the library and head south past Eddington to the path that runs from Wivenhoe Park to the village. I recognize the same tree that I passed out against the night Julie and I broke up. I haven't been here since. Claire and I chat about exams to pass the time and she asks me more questions about Italy.

We reach the café in Wivenhoe. It's one of those places that serves a full traditional English breakfast in the morning; bacon, eggs, baked beans, tomatoes, mushrooms, and sausage, fried up to a crisp with toast on the side to soak up the excess grease. I remember Chris knocking back a breakfast like that after a heavy night of drinking in Newcastle, while I struggled with tea and toast, trying not to vomit whenever I gazed at the repulsive fry up on Chris' plate.

Fortunately Claire and I just have coffee.

"Tell me something about Ireland. Have you lived there your whole life?" I ask.

"Why yes I have. I feel like I'm on a chat show now. What do you want to know Mr. Drew?"

This is her silly side I found so endearing in Clacton.

"I don't know. Just tell me something."

"Well, I went to an all girls' school where we wore cute uniforms."

"Nice. I'm a sucker for that look."

"Naughty boy! I still fit in mine by the way."

"Any chance you might model it for me?"

"I just may, but only if you're a good boy."

She winks at me. Claire is a total flirt like Christine, but I don't sense any damage, just a free spirit.

I get refills at the counter, come back and sit down and admire her discreetly. I always thought she was cute. I relive the moment when we had the conversation at the Jesus and Mary Chain concert. I never realized how much she liked me. Claire must have felt slightly jilted when I tried to hit on Julie at the disco and then a few weeks later asked her more questions about Julie. It wasn't until Clacton that I realized that we had chemistry.

"Penny for your thoughts?" Claire asks.

"I was just thinking about what we were starting to talk about yesterday before Julie came in, how we were talking at that Jesus and Mary Chain gig. I picked the wrong girl, Claire. I should have gone for you instead of Julie."

"Do you really mean that?"

"Yes."

"I've always liked you so much. I was so jealous of Julie. She'd complain about how you always wanted to listen to music and go to gigs and kept saying how you needed to grow up."

"Am I that bad? I know I can be a slacker, but I'm reasonably responsible."

"You're all good in my book," she says with a smile. "I did warn you that Julie was very serious when you asked about her."

"And I should have listened."

"Well, we're here now. That's what's important."

The two of us start walking back to Essex. I take her hand. She doesn't stop me.

When we get to the path Claire says, "I really like you, Drew. I'm sad that we're going to go our separate ways."

"I am, too. I'm going to New York in the fall. What about you?"

"I don't have any plans yet. I know, total procrastinator, story of my life. I know I don't want to go back to Belfast though. My uncle owns a pub in Dublin and he says I can always work there. I could write some short stories, maybe even a novel, and just work in the pub. A low pressure Bohemian lifestyle sounds really nice right about now. He has this small guest house on his property in Killiney, where I can live rent free, but that's too far away from you... that is if you really meant what you said about choosing the wrong girl."

"I meant it. You don't know how close I came to kissing you in Clacton when we were lip synching to that Human League song. In retrospect, I wish I had."

"So what's stopping you now?"

"Absolutely nothing."

I pull her close and kiss her softly on the lips. I think the Wivenhoe Park landscape artist, Mr. Constable, would have approved.

THERE IS A LIGHT THAT NEVER GOES OUT

I'm lying in bed with Claire in my room at Eddington, Lloyd Cole's *Rattlesnakes* playing softly in the background; "Perfect Skin." Claire has perfect skin. Everything about her is perfect. We've only been an item for about forty-eight hours now, but it feels like I've known her much longer. The two of us just click in all the stereotypical 'right' ways and the sex is fantastic. Even the first time we made love, just after returning from coffee in Wivenhoe, felt completely natural.

Afterward, Claire kissed me and with honesty in her eyes said, "You make me feel like a natural woman."

"And she can quote Aretha Franklin, too. What can't you do Claire?" I feel dopey and in love.

She giggled. "I'm just being silly. I'm really happy."

I remember my first time with Christine when I felt more like a play thing than a partner. Julie just cried a lot and freaked me out. Third time was the charm.

The two of us have done nothing but eat, sleep and fuck for the last two days, as if we were on some cheap holiday in the sun. Everything she does endears me to her even more. I like it when she walks around in my t-shirts, wearing nothing else but panties (mostly black) and I don't mind when she goes through my magazines and cassettes, unlike with Julie who had this habit of provoking my spider sense. I don't want to change a thing about Claire and I'm pretty certain she feels the same about me. Time is ticking though. Claire's graduating in a month and I'm going back to the States.

As if reading my thoughts, Claire says, "I don't want to let you go. Why don't you come to Ireland with me?

Otherwise, I'm going to follow you to America. You're not leaving without me."

"I don't want to be without you. You can follow me anywhere. That is anywhere but Michigan. You'd go off me if we went there."

"Nothing would make me go off you. I love you too much for that. It sounds silly saying that so soon, but..."

"I know what you mean," I say, trying to finish her sentence. "I've thought I've been in love before, but there always seemed to be conditions attached to it. Lord knows, Julie tried to change me."

"I'm glad she didn't."

"Have you ever been in love?" I ask.

"I thought I was my first year here," replies Claire. "There was a guy who was a third-year who I saw for about six months. A London lad, who had hair like Morrissey..."

"Ah, don't they all!"

She laughs and continues. "I was quite smitten with him at first, but he turned out to a bit dull. He was one of those record collector types who liked talking about music more than actually listening to it. You know the type. Music's supposed to be fun. I like seeing bands and dancing to music; no need to over analyze everything like a scholar."

"I hope you don't think I'm like that."

"No, you're too passionate. You're not the analytical type, you know, like a professor."

"My dad's a professor," I laugh, "and my brother wants to be one."

"You're joking, right? My father teaches economics at Queen's University in Belfast."

"My old man teaches history. I never knew we had that in common. So do you have any overachieving siblings, too?"

"No, it's just me. My parents are very Protestant if you catch my drift."

"I'm half-Catholic and half-Protestant, but I pay zero lip service to either faith. I'm about as non-practicing as you can get."

"We can spend the rest our Sundays in bed and grow old together, then."

"That sounds nice." Even though I barely know her, the idea of long term commitment doesn't scare me.

"Anyway, back to what we were talking about," says Claire. "In my second year I went off the rails a bit and slept around a little. Not like a total slag or anything, but I was a bit of a tart if you can imagine that."

She gives me a cute apologetic grin and rolls her eyes. "This year I've just been lonely. There's been no one until you."

"I'm no saint either. Trust me. I've made a lot of dumb mistakes."

"I'm still pinching myself that we're together. I wonder if Julie knows about us?"

I hadn't thought about that. "I imagine one of the guys in my flat may have said something to someone. Essex isn't that big. I wouldn't put it past Dave."

"Neither would I. The girls in my flat all liked Julie, too. They'll think I'm sort of evil vixen when they find out."

"That's their problem. You're all that I care about right now."

"Snap," she says as she kisses me. "So how does Dublin sound, then? That is if you feel like taking a year off your life. You can always finish university later. You could write for *Hot Press*. It's not exactly *Melody Maker*, but it's not bad. I'm sure you could work at my uncle's pub, too. We can live in his guest house rent-free. It's nice and isolated. My uncle has a huge place on the Killiney Road about a quarter-mile inland and there's a little gate lodge right by the road where the footman used to live in ancient times. It's quite cute and we'd be very alone. Bono lives down the road, too! I'd even model my schoolgirl uniform for you."

"Dublin it is. I love you Claire."

"I love you too, Drew. Think we should get out of bed and get something to eat? It's almost 3:00."

"The Hex beckons."

SOMEONE SOMEWHERE IN SUMMERTIME

It's the fourth of July, but for the first time since high school I'm not in some field in Michigan drinking cheap beer with friends and watching the fireworks. I'm in Killiney, gazing at the Irish Sea from a prime vantage point on a cliff overlooking the bay.

Claire and I moved to the gate lodge on her uncle's property as soon as we finished our exams. We've been taking it pretty easy. Both of us have been working part-time at her uncle's pub; he was kind enough to get me sorted with a work permit to extend my ex-pat life.

Mostly I've been writing. Nick put me in touch with *Hot Press* and I've completed some assignments for them. I'm also going to start writing for *Spin*, just small reviews, but it's a start. My parents aren't happy that I decided to drop out of school, but for the first time in my life I'm not on their dime. I need some space and time.

My friends have all started new lives. Dan has an internship in Washington, D.C. and will start his final year at Georgetown in the fall. Alan and James have landed positions in London and share a flat in Croydon, while Chris has accepted an offer to be some sort of junior banking executive in Newcastle. The last anyone saw of Dave was when he got escorted out of his economics final exam, a piece of paper having fallen out of his sleeve on to the floor.

Johnny's back in New York. I just got a card from him. Competition Orange has signed to Caroline Records and they're in the studio working on their first album. He's been hanging out with Nick and I'm jealous. I don't want anyone else to become his best friend. The five months we spent together at Essex feel like a lifetime of happy memories and I wish that I could freeze those moments for eternity—forever now—but both of us have to move forward with our lives.

A few days before Johnny flew back home, the two of us made a pilgrimage to Brighton. Both of us had always wanted to go there since first seeing *Quadrophenia* and the quaint picturesque resort town did indeed turn out to be the perfect place for us to say goodbye to England.

We found a café overlooking the sea and just sat there, drinking endless cups of sugary tea.

"Man, this place is nice," said Johnny.

"No doubt," I said. "I wonder how different my life would have been if we had gone here instead of Essex?"

"I think about stuff like that, too. Like if I had gone on a different program to Spain last year, would I have met another girl like Sophia, or would I have had an entirely different experience?"

"I'm glad it turned out the way it did, but I feel guilty about not going to New York with you."

"You shouldn't. Claire is really cool. You guys seem right together. I had my doubts when you first told me about that crazy weekend you got together, but now that I know her, I can see what you see in her."

"Thanks, man," I said. "Glad you're on my side. My parents are so pissed that I'm not coming home."

"It's your life, man. Don't let anyone run it for you."

"I agree. I need to stay away for awhile. I'm scared that if I go back right now, I'll just sell out and become normal, you know."

"I worry about shit like that, too," said Johnny. "I think the key is to stay connected to something creative. That way even if you have to work for the man, you still have a passion."

I look out at the ocean and kiss Claire softly. I'm pretty buzzed. Claire and I had a few drinks at our local just before heading to the beach and I sunk a couple of Valiums when she wasn't looking. I managed to get a new prescription from a counselor at Essex just after PJ died. "It'll ease your nerves," said the shrink.

Down below we see Bono walking on the beach with an entourage. He lives in our neighborhood and we often see him out and about. At first I was in awe of Bono until one day I walked past his mansion and caught him raking leaves in leather pants and a fisherman's sweater. The moment was so surreal that it's hard to take him seriously anymore.

Claire waves from above, and, surprisingly, Bono and his group wave back.

"Looks like God approves," laughs Claire.

But I don't care what God thinks. I've got an interview with Bobby Gillespie in Dublin later this evening.

CPSIA information can be obtained at www.ICGtesting.com
Printed in the USA
BVOW01s1018140414

350288BV00003B/4/P

9 781937 513306